The Millstone Falls

Ken Decoteau

Books by Ken Decoteau

- *Seventh Wielder*

- *The Last Necromancer*

- *Knave of Wands*

Fallen Apples Series:

1. *Fallen Apples*

2. *Three Blind Mice*

3. *Around the Juniper Tree*

4. *The Millstone Falls*

5. *From the Ashes*

A Once and Future War: (Fallen Apples Universe)

1. *The Iron Brigade* (Set in 2047) (Available Fall 2025)

2. *The Fireside War* (Set in 2048) (Forthcoming)

Cover art by Vranjković Nemanja
ISBN 979-8-9994661-0-5 (paperback)
ISBN 979-8-9994661-1-2 (ebook)

Chapter 1

Wheels

"I am alive," Jason Richardson hissed those words into the muggy summer air of his temporary Columbus, Georgia apartment and took a deep breath. With a wave of pain expected and delivered, he levered his body up to something slightly resembling a sitting position, and then slid off the bed into the ready wheelchair.

Now almost three months from taking a long string of automatic small caliber rifle fire into his lower half, Jason had only started his long road to recovery. The upside was, at present time, he could stand. Well, sort of. Jason smiled for a moment before wheeling towards the bathroom. A partially covered form of a sleeping Melissa Long washed away a bit of the pain. The blonde army technician had been one of two enlisted soldiers who inadvertently played a part of kicking off the last several months of activities which put him and his employer into the proverbial crucible of the security contractor world.

It wasn't Melissa's fault that a little shoulder launched drone her team was troubleshooting failed and dropped from the sky on the wrong lands in the Maine mountains that February. Melissa had successfully redeemed herself by helping Refit and Design International (RDI) ensure that two shipping containers packed full of stolen and much more capable mid-sized prototype RQ-21B drones were sent to the bottom of the ocean.

Unlike the small reconnaissance drone, which started the drama, the stolen units were being actively prepared to launch first a biological payload, and then small yield nuclear weapons. Removing the drones and deployment systems from the table was a huge win for global security.

Jason and Melissa worked closely together through that adventure and had become friends. Nothing more happened because of a chemistry mismatch. Melissa had dropped by unplanned in her dress uniform after making the rank of E-5 rather than taking her connection home when she landed in Atlanta. As she put it: "just to check on him." Next thing he knew, they were ordering a pizza and watching 13 Hours of Benghazi on the couch. Jason wasn't the same man he had been, and Melissa had gotten tipsy. And then, well, friends did what friends do. Got friendly.

With that grin on his face from the reminder that other things beyond standing remained intact, Jason deftly clicked off the brakes and spun the tires. Raising himself up on the grab bar took some effort. As was the norm for the week, his left leg started shaking mid-way through the process of relieving himself. Jason stuck with it, completing the simple but manly act called peeing while standing up before slumping back into his chair with a sheen of sweat on his face and a nasty charlie-horse in his left calf.

After massaging out the muscle, he spun into the main living room space of the handicap-ready 1-bedroom and kicked his laptop alive from its dock that was plugged into three monitors on a plastic table thanks to a single online shopping adventure. After a quick check of timing, he slammed a K-cup into the coffee machine and refilled the canteen with water from the sink. One thing about having a metal frame under you, Jason noted, was the ability to carry things like extra water, a Glock 19, spare mags, flashlight and knife and first aid kit, were almost limitless.

Fluids sorted, and a banana selected for a snack, Jason logged into his laptop rigged to the wall of monitors and clicked into his first meeting a bit early.

"I am alive," Jason whispered again as he opened up his notes and ignored the pain radiating up his lower back that always seemed to be worse when he first bent in half to mold to a chair. "I am alive."

"Jason, good morning!"

The pleasant tones from Charlotte Marlow, the NSA project manager, always brightened his mood. While she was lost and confused in the technology side of things, her ability to run meetings and cultivate people was top-notch. "How's tricks?"

Jason couldn't hold the laugh playing through the prior night in his head. Some tricks had been performed.

"Peachy smooth." Jason glanced quickly behind him to make sure no bits of a dress uniform or related parts were visible in the frame. "Agenda for today changed? I haven't checked yet."

Charlotte waved it off. "No changes, Jason. Oh, hi Carl!"

Carl Harding, the lead from the unit in NSA's DevOps

assigned to this case, nodded his head and fiddled with his headset before speaking. "Hear ya. Morning, guys."

"So, what do we have?" Charlotte led off.

"Mixed bag from our side." Carl frowned. "We are still combing through the systems recovered from the 4510 Iron Horse at the Kentucky core fiber node facility which were stitched into the network by Ulysses Security. Unfortunately, we can't confirm anything at this outside two years past. We know some of the kit was installed seven years ago, can't uncover exact dates. The access credentials Jason and RDI could provide us cut through the encryption nicely to confirm issues in the more recent time frame. However, the absolute size of the data which went through that system means we can't paint a full picture."

"That was my fear as well," Jason checked his notes. "When the hardware went online, almost eight years ago, it had the capacity of intercepting only minutes of internet traffic for its harvesting per hour. Since that time, consider the search window to be almost a full hour every hour, with processing of certain filter terms and queries returning in seconds. The primary code prioritized packages based on DNS, with at the time most DNS traffic being unencrypted on port 53."

"You mentioned the code can now issue responses in seconds?"

"Correct." Jason clicked open a tab and shared it. "And yesterday, we found out how. They leveraged a farm in Azure Cloud with K40 Tesla Nvidia cards to do the number crunching. Anyone analyzing traffic at Microsoft would assume the project mined Ethereum or similar cryptocurrencies. Instead, they were building up and unraveling patterns. The goal wasn't to decrypt or crack the HTTPS traffic. The question this software answers relates to who, when and where traffic flowed. From that data lake, they had several goals. The most obvious and dangerous goal post was related to hotspots. Think things like specific Instagram feeds or YouTube videos. Viral live streams."

Jason glanced at the bedroom door and felt a smile warm his face. Melissa's first unwanted claim to fame was one of such streams from her team member.

"Similar to the DHS's circuit breaker reset feature on YouTube?" Charlotte asked.

Shaking his head and laughing again, "You mean, the one which doesn't seem to work when it's activated? I heard your office tried it on my friends in Kentucky and failed. Again."

"Humor her." Carl brushed his beard and then reached for a coffee mug.

"From what I've been told," Jason proceeded carefully. "Facebook maintains a feature which allows Homeland access to cut thirty minutes of data from a region. Think: never happened. Posts gone, history gone, etc. Fun part is, they paid almost three billion dollars to make the same functionality as an option behind the scenes with YouTube, Twitter/X, Signal, Discord, Slack, Instagram."

"Well, those companies took the money, mocked something, then... kept iterating so fast that the fun shutoff button never met objectives. Google's the worst at it, since they basically have no real centralized control anymore due to all the zero-trust networking techniques they used to make things durable both internally, and with cloud users. Which brings me to the hotspot theory. On the internet, at the core, addresses are everything. DNS is HOW that everything gets agreed to. The Kentucky kit fiddled with the most important part of that agreement. TTL. Sorry, Time To Live."

"And this crap that Ulysses installed ramps up to act like the original access cut never happened, messes with TTLs to make the quick flip ineffective and then also starts poisoning caches with random requests. Interfere with that, and the safety interlocks kick in, which stops the cut."

"What do you propose next? Can we learn anything more from their hardware?"

"I'd just kill it," Jason shook his head, thinking through how much the KT hardware cost to keep running in the NSA lab at an undisclosed location. "No real benefit to keeping them running. I'd pull the plug and shelve the hardware."

Jason looked over his shoulder to see Melissa's backside vanish into the bathroom. Carl grinned, seeing only a very brief flash of blonde hair and a sheet. Jason shrugged.

"Sorry, guys. Unexpected house guest. Tiny apartment."

Jason noticed Carl was rubbing his collar bone. The former competitive cyclist had commiserated with Jason offline when they started calls since Carl had taken a nasty spill at forty miles an hour and ended up with a broken femur and collar bone at the same time. Carl had passed him suggestions for food, acupuncturist schools of thought to look for, and how to find a good massage therapist.

Cut out the hot wings and beer, and replace it with lots of steamed veggies and ginger were solid take-aways from that knowledge share which Jason had been honoring. Seeing a girl in the young man's space made Carl feel better about the chances of Jason's recovery. Sometimes, everyone needed company.

"Now, on to the next ticket," Marlow flipped a page in her notebook. "Is the functional review complete of the reporting code?"

"Ah, yes. Event reviews. We have two completed review simulations with the software," Jason opened up a slide deck. "We are waiting on data transfer and releases for the rest of the events. First, let me take you back to February 2010. Libyan people essentially took over their own country, and as the entire cellular phone system there goes through one company, and the NSA already had the entire record set, it was rather easy to crunch. This slide is level 1, essentially a clumping analysis. The algorithm is straight out of crowd analysis using behavioral assessments. This produced a clear mapping of the two primary sides of the conflict. We focused on the February 17th martyrs. Since we know their roster well, we can corroborate how close the algorithm matched reality. Left is, guessed; right is actual. This shows about 90% overlap. Software guessed some bad guys were good guys."

"Also note, this gives an organizational map. While not completely correct, the produced org chart was darn close, only flipping a few mid-level staff around. All twenty-three primary leadership were correctly identified."

"Level 2 assesses how sensitive the person is to influence. The color blue shows stable status, as in don't bother. Yellow indicates high chance to, er, leverage? I guess leverage is the correct term, right, Carl?"

The man gave a little laugh at the dig and shrugged.

"This last slide is a snapshot from almost a year later.

BAM, five of twenty-three who were marked as yellow targets have left the organization. Also, all extra ones the software showed incorrectly for membership in 17th Feb transitioned to blue members of 17th Feb."

"Interesting," Carl nodded. "Seems pretty good, from one case."

"Flipping to case two, this is that recent election result protest day," Jason spoke carefully, but Carl still raised an eyebrow and held up a hand.

"Um, that's not something I'd have expected you to have access to, Jason."

"I'm covered. The RDI Florida team consulted with a component of that investigation and had the phone data." Jason flipped the slide. "Level 1 run indicated... this..."

The slide showed blobs of ones and twos together, but almost no connecting lines.

"Two things to point out. First, as you see, not much clumping going on here. We thought the cause was a higher percentage of people, roughly 42% vs the 5% in Benghazi, were using HTTPS for DNS. So we looked at another grouping method."

The slide flipped to a complete org chart map with around thirty people. "This includes four members of the police, a handful of Uber drivers, some staff members, and at the top, this guy who trains actors. Several of them are in the yellow group. Follow me so far?"

"And this result was without the actual contents of the DNS requests? Just from the fact that requests were made?" Marlowe asked.

"Yes..." Jason deflected. He had some of query contents,

but RDI wasn't ready to release that dataset to Homeland yet, if ever.

"Okay, what next?"

"The theory we're working on is going to be tough to run down, and it'll likely require another proposal."

Jason shook his head and killed the presentation before continuing. His face showed the pain the death of his friend, Scott Rupp, brought to the surface. The man had died to get them this information.

"The enemy team in Kentucky which hit us at RDI was going to be upgrading the servers. That extra boost in processing power would increase the effectiveness of that deployment. I must note, though, that the older model simply isn't all that useful anymore. The Iron Horse installation was only tapping into a single DNS communication path, and thus it was likely getting only a small subset of the quality of data it really needed to shine. Maybe 1/10th. And second, I'm pretty sure you guys have systematically searched for and taken out these hard-to-manage physical installations. Like I started with, this was what looks like a generation 1 proof-of-concept. Our bet is these guys are on gen 6."

"And that might be?"

Jason held up his phone.

"Pretty simple, Carl. If you follow the crumbs everyone brings with them as they strengthen their code and tool-boxes," Jason opened up a game. "Know all these free games, services, and apps with ads?"

"Ya, my daughter can't stop playing Farmville."

"Bingo! The point of those apps is not to give a person a chance to have a good time. It's harvesting data. You are the product. Why do you think even paid apps always provide a path to play that doesn't require money? Everyone knows data goes to all kinds of places. From the makers of the applications to advertising firms and marketing analytics silos. We're pretty sure some of that data is being slurped into a massive data lake managed by the same bad guys who installed these servers. Also, that more recent versions of this 4510 codebase prototype are being executed against that data lake. Now it's not limited to using what the software could harvest across the wire through physical interception."

"Which app is it?" Carl narrowed his eyes.

Shrugging, Jason locked his phone and took a sip of water.

"Could be any of them. Could be all of them. No easy way to tell, hence a separate proposal to analyze further. We'd need data, massive amounts of data. A couple of big data analysts and likely machine learning experts. And even then, I'm not sure we can figure it out. Hence my second suggestion."

"That is?"

"I don't know yet, still working it out. We know going to HTTPS DNS helps reduce the effectiveness of this software, and uninstalling silly games helps, but much of the benefit of this software is in the data that leaks from other devices. It's not just enough to lock down the phones of our people. We'd have to lock everyone down they come in contact with. If their daughter, sister, brother, boyfriend or a random dude walking his dog while you're out for a jog are near you with any of the data gathering logic onboard and active, this software should be able to identify a meaningful picture of your life in that encounter."

"In conclusion, then?" Marlowe asked. "We wrap this up in the next week, and then review two new projects?"

"I'm thinking that's what it will take. One team to see if they can get anything out of that free data theory, and a second to figure out a way to fight back."

"All right," Jason tapped his mouse. "I think I'm done here for RDI. Anything else?"

"Don't forget to fill out your time card for the project!" Charlotte said.

The reminder in place, they all signed off the call.

Chapter 2

Port

"All right boys," Olivia Kuznetsov lifted her sunglasses off of her blonde hair and dropped them over her nose. Giving a theatrical wave to the laptop resting against her thighs under the shade completed the show. "We're all done here. Don't forget to fill out any paperwork you need to before Elizabeth comes and finds you with a trocar and a bucket. That includes time cards!"

"Yesh," Fat Al rolled his eyes in the video feed. Justin Tarbert slapped his arm and muted their feed.

Laughing, as Al Smith was always a prankster, Olivia killed the call and closed the laptop. Relaxing back in the lounge chair, she closed her eyes to assess. She let the light sea breeze mingle with her thoughts, and the smell of the tropical ocean clear her mind.

Olivia thought carefully about whether she should put on another coat of sunscreen, or just hope for the best. She had fifty more laps to do in the pool before switching gears and getting ready for the next planning meeting on Tori Station with the base commander and Army Criminal Investigation

(CID) folk.

Three months in Okinawa set her late thirties toned body up with the best tan of her life. She had kipped home twice to make sure her cat was okay and deal with administrative drama. Her damn furry critter had all but adopted Hong Nori Lin's daughter as his new favorite person. The elderly ball of claws and spit deserved some stability. Fortunately, the seven-year-old Asian-Irish redhead girl, Wei Song, was being well-schooled by the cat in the proper ways of having a soul which was predisposed to mischief.

Glancing around briefly, Olivia verified no one was around the pool area of the former Airbnb villa they had rented when their watch on the island started three months ago. Now that property was owned by Refit and Design International (RDI). They had settled in hard to the location as a one of two bases of operation for their current mission.

Two doors down on the beachfront, they had a second, larger house. That one didn't have the outstanding pool, and this one didn't have enough beds for their teams. Thus, the boys got the larger domicile and the girls, currently her and fellow security contractor Cynthia Wiggins, had this one to themselves. Olivia untied her top, reached up and dropped the canopy which had been necessary in the South China Sea summer sun to work the laptop screen, and rolled over to sun her back.

Her thoughts went towards their past. Almost five months of turmoil, and now she was splitting her time between sunbathing, swimming, and kicking the asses of her team as they were ... waiting. Waiting for permission to move on the enemy.

This was the longest Olivia ever sat on a damn point and just chilled her "toes and goes," as her aunts had called that chaotic combination of vibrational energy which had gotten her into so much trouble as a child. Every day, she briefed the RDI team with a status update. Every other day, she hopped into a meeting with the joint chiefs and some spooks to review the status of their updates on the investigation. Her people kept getting stalled.

The issue was obvious to Olivia. There was a 320 ft long ship doing laps in the Southern Pacific around a six-day steam away from her while a machine shop in its belly was churning out compact nuclear warheads. Those were actively being sold or traded for nasty things in unsavory ways. That ship had to die; and RDI had the remote control and was ready to change the channel.

Olivia checked her watch to make sure the alarm was set so she could snag a shower before the meeting with the joint chiefs. After a sip of water, she laid her face down on a towel and decided the laps could wait until after a nap since she'd been splitting time zones across the world for weeks.

"Winks, then workout."

Chapter 3

Hammer

Brian Deegan felt every one of his thirty-two years of age as he struggled to get the 6 x 6 inch, 14 foot beam level. Finally, twisting enough to pass his threshold for faking the bubble, he zipped in two screws.

The weight off his body, he sighed, relaxed back on the top of the ladder, and then glared at his level as he realized he would need to make an adjustment. The screw he'd used to block the opposite end of the heavy beam was too low, and... He wasn't as good at precision wood working as he had wished. Watching YouTube only got you so far in the real world with imperfect wood, uneven surfaces, and a battered body.

Brian wiped sweat from his brow with the dusty back of his hand, dropped his square back in the tool belt, and began to carefully climb down off the ladder to get some scraps of wood he could use to brace the board and attempt to fix his mistake. While four hands would be better than two for setting beams, the last thing he was going to do was ask his current house guest, Molly Turner, to climb up a ladder and lift crap over her head the day before her twenty-fifth birthday.

Just in the foothills of the Appalachian range, north and east of Atlanta, Georgia, the forty-acre homestead had been in his family since forever. His aunt turned it from little more than a notorious moonshine shack into what amounted to a small farm with a quaint and sturdy house. Her greenhouses and canning resources were deep and stood proud against the test of time following her passing.

The smell of jasmine and azalea rode across the clearing on the muggy winds which swept up the slops of the land. It was hot and humid, as always in the early summer weeks after the spring rains.

Things were in good repair, even though Brian had only a limited presence at the home for the last few years. He'd given the chickens over to the neighbors a long while back, and the goats had found better pastures with more present owners to provide them snacks.

To him, it was home.

Three months before, he had invited his friend, Molly Turner, to "temporarily" stay with him for a few days as they were both discharged from a "Special Hospital" in Columbus, Georgia. Since their arrival at that government run medical facility had been via one of the President's Own VK34 helicopters with a full Marine platoon in guard, that neither were active duty soldiers was ignored. To find their friend, Jason Richardson, also at the same facility and miraculously alive following a horrific few hours and a sketchy nine-line helicopter evacuation helped both feel better about what they had survived.

Getting the critically injured man to safety had not been easy for them. Both Brian and Molly had been shot to shit. Not anywhere near as bad as what Jason had experienced the day before Molly initiated a live-stream last stand at a highschool field in Kentucky, but bad.

After a few days of break from the hospital process at the Georgia farm, the two of them had enacted one of his aunt's grand plans for the homestead. He felt like somewhere in their current action was a motive brewing in his brain, but it was a good plan either way. They couldn't go back to serious security contractor work for a while and needed something to do.

A few years before her passing, Auntie Evaline Deegan had paid an architecture firm to design a master bedroom suite to be added onto the small old home. Her stipulation was a testament to her upbringing. She refused to play games. All construction plans were paid for up front. All materials ordered, delivered, and stored.

At her low rate of income, it would take at least five years after those resources were laid in for her to recover that nut so that she could pay for the labor for a crew to do the work. She didn't manage that before passing away. Brian, with his big brain, defensive end build, and idiotic sense of timing, talked Molly into helping him start the addition on their own. He figured at some level, the work would be a way to focus on healing.

"You know," Molly spoke softly from behind him. He hadn't heard her walk up. "It helps to have a second person for the heavy stuff."

Brian accepted a glass of lemonade. While not homemade

like his aunt had produced in five gallon jugs, Molly had taken to picking some up from the local farmer's market. It was a compromise. He preferred sweet tea, and she normally drank coffee all day. Lemonade, light on the sugar, was an option they both could stomach.

"Thanks." Brian took a sip and thought about ignoring the jibe, about not asking her for a hand. Looking down at her right forearm, which was still in a cast because of taking a round through her wrist, and knowing her right shoulder wasn't up for much more than lifting a coffee cup on some mornings, Brian sighed and moved to set up the second ladder.

"Our deal was that we'd both get work in building back up our strength," Molly grabbed a speed square and an impact driver from the tool bucket and checked the battery charge and direction.

Once she was settled on the ladder, Brian went back to his side and loosened the end, giving Molly the slack needed to make the adjustment. She expertly levered the board in place with a framing hammer wedged against a screw, checked the square, tweaked the board slightly more and zipped it in, giving him a nod to finish his side.

"Anything more about the new project you might move to?"

"Not much yet," Molly shook her head. "Hawk Works has been tight-lipped about it. I just know that it's medical research. From the specs, likely a gene sequencing thing. Cancer research maybe, or drug interaction modeling. They've got some clients in both spaces, and either category could use something like the server room full of hardware they want my help with."

"Don't you still have time left on the helicopter project with Sikorsky through RDI?"

Molly nodded and then accepted the end of the last beam from Brian. She zipped in a pair of screws to hold the weight while he transferred himself and the other ladder to the right location. "Technically, another three months, and they look to be extending. However, I've been a bit bored. The initial month was hell. Well, not just because I was in the hospital for a solid chunk of it and spending all day on a computer sucked. The needs from a DevOps Engineer role like myself were actually pretty basic once I got my head around the wacko way of Google's cloud platform. Since I seemed bored, the lead asked if I'd be willing to spend some time assessing this other project and maybe move there when the helicopter control telemetry overlay thing finishes this phase."

"Instead of coming to RDI?" Brian asked hesitantly.

In February, she had joined Brian's former company, Ulysses Security, along with Olivia and Collin Duez as a technical operations contractor. Her role had been a mix between a shooter and a geek. Modern contractor teams had been moving towards embedding experts to bridge the gap between grunt and silicone. That transition had given people like Molly, who loved to shoot and had a degree in computer science and engineering, a place to contribute beyond the IDPA and 3-Gun matches she had excelled at.

After a nasty string of events, his entire team left Ulysses for RDI. Molly, however, had been slightly stuck by a non-compete clause on her contract until her former employer had tried to have her killed. Twice.

"Do you regret coming down here to Georgia?" Brian watched her swat at a mosquito. "Instead of staying in Connecticut near the Hawk Works office?"

"Brian..."

Molly sighed and winced slightly as she struggled with aligning the beam edge, and almost dropped the hammer. It was hard to hold it in the cast.

"You didn't ask me that for the first month. Recently you've been asking about it once a week. What's next? Daily? Every time I almost drop something?"

"And you mostly avoid giving an honest answer while we have been finishing this section," Brian then pointed his screw gun at the partially framed expansion. The little corner they had just added beams to was going to be a covered patio area which extended past the exterior edge. The core framing was completed, and they were going to be putting the roof on in the next few days.

"I need to sit down anyway," Molly lowered the screw gun, knocked the hammer off the ladder in the process and climbed down.

Brian followed her to the picnic table under the large live oak tree, also the coolest corner of the open yard. Molly laid down on one bench with a sigh and a groan at the stretch, took a few deep breaths, raised to a sitting position, and glared at the large man. He paused at the look, a glass of lemonade halfway to his lips, and then set it down fast enough that a few drops splattered the old wood.

"My original intention with the Hawk Works contract," Molly spoke slowly and calmly, but Brian could hear some of the pain echoing through her voice. "Was to recover from being shot up and beaten up in Baku. I figured six months was enough time to get the stupid employment situation resolved and get myself back to some form of operation. I really know I want to do more than just stare at a screen all day and night. Even though the experience thus far has been traumatic."

"And now," she continued, before he could make a complaint, her right hand in the air. "I know I don't need to remind you of my punch list for holes and problems. Just like you don't need to remind me of how badly you got dinged up. Also, I noticed you haven't been taking all of your meds for that kidney. And you are frequently pushing yourself out here when I'm heads-down in computer crap so that I don't have as much to do each day. That isn't helping either of us."

"So, yes, Brian, I may not be going back to RDI when the Hawk gig finishes. I'll chat with Olivia and Trevor and take their input when I decide. I'll also chat with you." She softened from her glare to a more gentle smile. "I'll also be chatting with you about it. Now, part two."

Molly waved around the homestead.

"Other than the internet sucking occasionally, and having to put up with the fact that you keep leaving the damn toilet seat up, I am very well fed and I don't mind doing dishes. And along that line, I had to ask you something today, anyway."

Brian raised an eyebrow, suddenly reminded of being lectured on the same table when he was a teenager over a situation involving a .22 bolt-action rifle and a neighbor's barn.

"It's June 9th. I have to decide today whether I'm taking Hawk Works's relocation package." Molly announced. "I had almost forgotten there was one until Olivia reminded me using big winky emoji and purple bunny rabbits bouncing all about in her texts."

"I..." Brian hadn't expected the conversation to go this way. "Um, where?"

"Here," Molly resumed her glare, struggling to keep her expression stern. "Here; Navy. You understand the words I am speaking, no?"

"I don't know," Brian stalled for time, but smiled internally at the familiar tone. "How much stuff are we talking about here? Collin and I moved Olivia once up from Pennsylvania to New Hampshire. It was a nightmare."

Molly raised an eyebrow and felt her cheeks color slightly.

"The only thing I care about that's not already down here with me right this minute is a shoe box with all the Crayons you and Collin kept shoving in my face while we were in Azerbaijan. Most of the furniture was just crap I picked up from yard sales or GoodWill."

"There's a part two in there," Brian narrowed his eyes and leaned forward, resting his elbows on the table, considering her expression carefully. "I can tell you have a second point to the topic."

"I have two choices, Brian. Option A: I admit I don't know how to move, and they contract for a company to come in, pack me up and deliver my kit. All of that junk is already sitting in a storage locker in New Hampshire. Option B: I take a lump sum and say I will handle the move myself. Or something. But I have to change my physical address."

"So, presuming, for the time being, that I grudgingly grant you my permission to officially change your residence to my place," Brian tried to keep a straight face as Molly leaned back and crossed her arms, challenging him to continue. "You would receive a chunk of cash?"

"Correct," Molly nodded, uncrossed her arms and pointed with her left hand to the large garden, which other than having a few Sunflowers and some leftover ground cherries, sage and garlic which volunteered to stay from the prior years, was overgrown with weeds. "I know we'd talked about it, but the addition to the house took priority for a few reasons and we sort of got distracted. Not complaining about that, because it's gotten way hotter fast. We still got distracted."

"I could rent a tiller?"

Brian had tried the mechanical one in the barn, but realized quickly it required some horsepower.

"Or we could get a horse and use the other old stuff in the barn, too." Molly had joked that she'd have to put a harness on him for the decades-old tiller to be useful. "Alternatively, I could buy a tractor and some implements."

"Buy and not rent?"

They rented a skyjack which was being delivered the coming week to help with the roof, but he hadn't considered a purchase of any equipment. As someone who was away from home for 3 weeks out of every 4 for several years, his perspective hadn't thought buying was an option.

"Why not?" Molly. "We nearly killed each other while cutting down one of those twisted trees last month. I've been thinking about it for a while, and I believe it'll be a game changer. Between knocking out the garden and moving all the soil to finish the landscaping around the addition, not to mention clearing the field on the other side of the stream. Why not?"

"So, what you're really asking is for a place to, what, store your tractor?" Brian went back to his deadpan expressionless delivery, which was his way of setting up a tease. "How big are we talking here? Said hypothetical tractor?"

"Brian," Molly sighed. "May I move in with you?"

He leaned back and laughed, got up and sat down next to her, and gave her a hug. "Hey, why not? I'll even let you buy me a tractor."

"My tractor, Navy!" Molly spoke into his shoulder, doing her best not to let her laughter and sense of relief get into her voice. "My tractor. Get it right."

Chapter 4

Docks

"I think we're going to need a bigger tractor," Trevor Sanders frowned at the scene on the sweltering tropical docks in Kaohsiung, Taiwan. He was tapping a clipboard against his thigh and watching a large forklift and a little blue tractor with forks on its loader attempt to coordinate the pick of a 40 foot shipping container off a truck.

Lots of shouts and frantic hand gestures bounced between two of the port crew, the operators, and the two small men attempting to guide the equipment. The men were all dressed in button down white shirts and jeans. The clothing was the local uniform of choice, even in the 110 degree heat at 0600 local time.

Trevor stood tall, just over the six-foot mark, and had the build of a long time athlete. As the northeast regional operations manager for RDI, he had an entire office of three teams under his technical responsibility. While he couldn't run fast, he could run long. And pushing nearer to 50 years old than he regularly admitted, his careful maintenance of self, other than his diet when his wife wasn't home, did not yet show. He still knew his limits, and he needed backup for this particular container of cargo.

Trevor turned to a recent RDI hire, Collin Duez. The man was about ten years younger and under the around 5 foot 11 in boots. The wiry man, a former Navy Special Warfare Combatant-craft Crewmen (SWCC), looked absolutely miserable in the sun. Collin bore all the telltale signs of too much baby powder scented sunscreen around his exposed damp edges.

Collin also wore an extremely faded baseball cap from Tennessee Tech. Trevor, much more experienced in the ways of sketchy port operations, had packed his very own wide-brimmed hard hat and had a bandanna zip-tied into the back to cover all of his ears and neck. That cloth was also still thawing from where he had left it in the freezer overnight after soaking it in water. Just because he was black, didn't mean he was going to pick a fight with the sun.

Trevor passed Collin a water bottle from his daypack. "Should we offer to help?"

Collin chugged the bottle, savoring the momentary relief delivered by the chilled water. "Why? It's not technically our gear. Also, I feel like I'm literally swimming in this air."

Captain Wayne Bright, the master of the *Sandy Stewart*, the small ship tied up directly behind them, crossed his arms and shook his head. "Tell me again, why again do I not want to put this load directly onboard, Trevor?"

Trevor snorted, raised the clipboard and read through the form one more time. Collin was technically right. It wasn't their gear at all. The contents were property of the United States Navy. Or "had once been" as they were about to all get "lost at sea in a boating accident" in a logistics department memo before the next audit.

"Because, until I sign for it, it's not our problem. I emphatically told the port agent I would not do that until the load was off the trailer, on the ground, intact customs seal verified and snipped with witnesses on camera, and THEN inspected for damage. You don't want to touch the shipment. It has HAZMATS."

"I read the manifest." Bright let a laugh escape as the little tractor tipped up a bit as the forklift guy went down too fast. "Pucker factor engaged right then for that guy!"

"The manifest isn't the manifest." Trevor spoke softly and didn't look over at the captain.

"Oh."

"Which is why I wanted to make sure and give you complete awareness of the contents before you touch the damn thing. If you refuse, I will respect that."

The captain walked away towards his ship without a word for Trevor. The experienced man knew the unsaid command was just that. A command. *Follow. Now.*

While a violation of several international laws had been made in shipping that container, those who made those laws sometimes skirted them. A placard was present in its proper holders and the forms showed the same. However, the most dangerous component inside weren't the lithium batteries contained in equipment signified by the four-digit code on the hazardous materials placard.

Trevor followed the captain onto the worn deck, past massive rigging, and around to the starboard side and then into a locker. Noting its contents, he quickly realized it was the

Bosun's locker. The single place where everything needed to run the ship's deck went through. Broken, bent, or dirty; you would find what you needed there to make anything right. You also touched nothing without permission from the hand who ran the deck, the Boatswain.

Once inside the Bosun's locker with the hatch dogged and the smell of fish bait and grease locked into the small space between them, Trevor carefully and calmly rested against a bench to make his pitch.

"The container outside holds thousands of pounds of explosives of various flavors and fragrances. Everything from C4 to SMAW rounds, to a stack of Russian manufactured anti-ship mines."

"And what in the hell makes you guys think I'd for a moment let munitions like that on my ship? I knew roughly we're picking up some jar heads or swimmers, and boats, and going on a little hunt. No one told me you were planning on blowing up something."

"Captain," Trevor kept his calm, though he wished the light sea breeze he had been enjoying outside was coming through the door and clearing the air of the compounded odors. "Are you familiar with the 77th Infantry Division? They formed in World War II."

"Not personally."

"When things were ramping up to get the United States into war footing, the army performed an experiment by lumping a bunch of old dudes in their own unit together and running them through basic training. Average age was 33, the oldest in his 50s."

"Go on."

"Couple things. First, most brand new units at the time were young and fresh, the bulk of them under 23. Every war game the 77th did against those new units resulted in the young folk being crushed. Literally crushed. How?" Trevor pointed to his clipboard. "Old age and treachery. See, captain," Trevor paused as the door opened and then slammed shut with a clank and screech, punctuating an entrance of a small man.

"Trevor Sanders, Bosun," Bright nodded at the wiry old guy. His face was so weather scared, Trevor did not know whether he was 50 or 90. Though small of frame, his forearms were the size of tree trunks. The newcomer did not offer a hand in greeting.

"Keep going."

"On December 9th, 1944, a day after successfully taking a Japanese-held harbor as part of one of the most contested islands in the Philippines, the 77th ambushed an enemy troop carrier in the middle of the night. To this day, they are the only infantry unit credited with sinking a naval vessel. Why this matters a bit to us is, we are a company of old men, like the 77th. For them, there was no desire for fame from the vessel kill, or even recognition for anything else they did. They were driven to get crap done, and go take a nap back home. The 77th were vital in taking Okinawa, and much of this region back."

"In a similar fashion, because of our dad-nap being taken from us by someone actually dropping two bombs on our heads, we're here with our old man, mad dad energy. And we are planning to not play along with the rule set. We are also, however, playing things very safe."

Bosun sniffed, uncrossed his arms to yank a pair of bolt cutters off a hook, and then unlocked the door and waved Trevor out. Pushing off the bench, Trevor inhaled deeply the moderately fresher harbor air.

Back off the ship, the pair of operators had finally managed the tumultuous dance to mostly not drop the heavy container. With the locals heading back to the warehouse row, Bosun went over and snipped the tag. Door open, Trevor went in with a flashlight lit and Collin on his elbow to begin their inspection.

Ten minutes later, the bosun gathered his crew, hopped in the crane's doghouse on the ship, and began the process of carefully taking the container on board. Collin remained to help, and Trevor followed the captain up to a small office behind the bridge. The stark contrast from the sweltering sauna outside to the 72 degrees F conditioned space made Trevor shiver.

Bright sat at his desk and reached for a can of diet coke. "Old age and treachery, you said? Why necessary? We've worked with the Seals and DEVGRU teams before on some projects. Why am I talking to you, and not some hot shot major?"

"Because I was a hotshot major, and I trained scores more in the art and the faith." Trevor took the other chair, dropping his hard hat into his lap. "This doesn't leave this room, except for the bosun. I could tell you two have a dual-role running a ship, and we checked on your record carefully before picking you out of the hat."

"I'll have to tell the chief engineer some things," the Captain warned.

Trevor held up a hand. "Please pick carefully. We're committing a bit of a shell game here because the bad people who we are after likely have access to most, if not all, facility documentation. Both commercial ports, and military bases. If we officially left Taiwan heading into their Area of Operations with a container full of, and believe me, they have their eyes on us, that sort of material out there, likely they would panic. It's taken a lot of effort to track down our target. People died for this. As you likely guess, it's not the UAV recovery we contracted your ship for that is our mission. Oh, there is a UAV, and we will pick it up. It was sent out here, so we'd have a reason to come collect it on paper."

"Go on."

"We will probably have to board teams out of customs without official documentation. Our primary mission goal is to send a ship to the bottom of the ocean as a twisted pretzel."

"I appreciate the direct approach, Trevor," Bright leaned forward and set his hands on his desk. "I also can tell you believe what you are about is the right play. Just give me something to sway me over. As short as possible."

Trevor opened his phone and keyed up a video of Molly Turner and a cab driver in Azerbaijan, tossing a nuclear warhead into the back of a bloody pickup truck in front of a restaurant.

"Looks like a mortar round," Bright passed back the phone.

"It's a nuke."

"Did that hit an ATM machine? It had been launched?"

"The machine absorbed the final kinetic energy, yes. We got it before it could arm. Fortunately, they used a reliable modern trigger system on the warhead."

"Russian?"

"They aren't stupid about nukes. This one product is worse in its origin. Modern dark commercial market." Trevor shook his head and tapped the clipboard three times with his index finger. "This delivery of snacks is to ensure the next one, or ten, doesn't end up clicking off over a football game or a parade or worse."

"Shit. Really?" The blood drained from the captain's face and he leaned back.

"Now you know why we're here." Trevor let himself relax. "We are reeling in a fish. Our hook is already quite set."

"The 77th you said? Old man, mad dad energy?" Bright snickered a little at Trevor's serious nod. "Bosun's Charlie, by the way. Him and I are in. I'll figure out something to tell the chief engineer. He's good, but doesn't need to know much more than to keep his crews out of that container for security reasons. He will geek."

"Look up that unit's history. Lost of good learning from their tale. Makes us old guys feel better about our chances of survival in the world."

"One last question, Trevor," Bright tapped the table three times at the same tempo Trevor had used against the clipboard. "As a mariner first, and a man of faith; can you assure me that getting the crew off that ship before twisting it into that pretzel you desire is in your mission plans?"

"This is going to sound like a joke. A Marine and a Navy Seal got together with an Army Engineer and concocted this little thing, which makes certain modern ships go a bit crazy. They call it The Thang. And we have one of those little systems already onboard our target vessel. Getting the crew off will not be too hard. That is actually our first milestone."

"I've heard that name before. Wasn't there a tank in Vietnam nicknamed that? My dad was a Marine there."

"Yup, the Ontos. Bazooka tank. Our *Thang* doesn't turn buildings into rubble while looking absolutely badass. It instead messes with ship systems in rather unfortunate ways for her crew. The name has everything to do with how it functions, psychologically. Just like with the Ontos, our device is capable of scaring the shit out of the target."

"Good enough for now, Trevor," Bright shook his head, still processing the full conversation. "Nukes? Really?"

"Fallen Apples from the Tree of Knowledge, in the wrong hands; that they are." Trevor shrugged. "Oh, and don't use those terms either. Some people in Washington think they are really clever for coming up with code words like Fallen Apples for this crap. Straight out of the oldest story pertaining to the origin of humanity."

Bright laughed. "I never understood politics. Those guys always seem to think they have some special magical thread to sell."

"We're not here to weave, Captain Bright. We're here to drop a millstone on foreheads. Let's go hunting."

Trevor opened a second phone he had set up just for their final preparations. He tapped out a simple text to his boss, MD; "Your Uber Driver picked the takeout you ordered up. On the way!"

Chapter 5

Order Up

"Are you actually going to place an order for BattleBoxes this time, Josiah? Or are you going to keep teasing us with additional clauses, software requests for features? Or does your boss, Clint, need another pair of fuzzy bunny slippers?" Jason rested back in his chair and massaged out a cramp in his left leg.

"Bad one there?" Josiah Richter noted the wince and shift of Jason in the frame of the video call. As an after-effect of Josiah, and his boss, Clint Gray at Rose Armaments, helping Jason get out of a potential ambush safely months back, the two of them had set up a weekly check in.

While the massive defense contract company Rose was completely above the board, the scuttlebutt and the easy impression was that Josiah entertained a dual-role as an advisor and card-carrying member of The Central Intelligence Agency. While Jason had nothing but respect for this assumed CIA resource, he also knew to hold his cards close and not count his money at the table.

"It sucks sitting in a chair all day." Jason let his leg go

and waved at the face of Josiah in a small window on his laptop screen to the right side of the desk. The two monitors in the center were both large screens and full of code, work tickets, merge request reviews, and to his latest horror, a stack of resumes. They were hiring. "Also, you didn't answer my question about buying more communications hardware. Which is it?"

"Let's say we barter for another round of 150 boxes; 50 large, and 100 with the smaller cases. All with batteries."

Jason looked at his calendar, which was almost full enough to require a monitor of its own, and then checked his text messages.

"I had been hoping to catch lunch with someone before they fly out," Jason frowned and set the phone down. "I will not have enough time with you playing games. All right, what do you have in mind for an exchange?"

"I offer forth a name," Josiah lifted a yellow legal pad and flipped to a page, and then showed a hand written splatter of blobs and lines. The blobs each had a tiny text in them, and all pointed up towards one large oval. Josiah spoke the name out loud, which he tapped with the tip of a pencil. "James Weatherly."

"Is that an organization map?"

Jason had seen Trevor and Olivia pouring over something closely resembling the same pattern on a dry-erase board a few times. It looked like a tableau out of a crime movie; when the hero investigator reveals a hidden truth.

"Mr. Weatherly is, or kind of was, I guess, the chief security officer for Ulysses. On paper anyway. Thus, of course he had, on paper, been on the top of everyone's list as someone who might be in the full know of, well, security things." Josiah waved a chicken wing in front of his camera and took a bite. "These are good. Garlic Parmesan! Best flavor, or the worst flavor; depending. The cheese to oil ratio has to be carefully metered."

Jason pursed his lips at the reminder that he was now likely missing lunch with Melissa Long. "Not helping. How did this Weatherly CSO guy get passed by on the first glance? Yet he was significant after all? Assuming I'm hearing you correctly?"

Josiah finished inhaling the chicken wing and wiped his face with a bandanna. "Yeah. So, this Weatherly guy looked from the outside like a complete corporate rockstar. The critter would have 10-12 hours of meetings on his calendar, 6 days a week. Thing is, they were all useless crap. Meetings about having meetings to schedule other meetings or retrospectives about meetings."

Josiah sipped a tall pilsner and smacked his lips theatrically.

"On deep dive, patterns emerged. Weatherly was all fake. His presence was just a show to make it look like he was putting on the usual expected corporate peacock dance. Some poor executive assistant somewhere was likely given the full-time job of orchestrating the facade. Took a while to see through it, and we likely wouldn't if a person frequently attending those silly meetings hadn't messed up their time card."

"How so?" Jason asked, crossing his arms and setting back in his chair. He was completely convinced that Josiah was playing with him. Not about the story he was telling, but by eating greasy fried food and drinking beer; both of which were not on Jason's recovery diet plan.

"It's rather hard to believe a smoke show of a project director would simultaneously be in a four-hour retro on a corporate roll-out of binary authorization for their container images while also attending her best friend's daughter's wedding. It wasn't easy, but we unraveled some veritable balls of yarn from that lead. Funny, we likely wouldn't have uncovered the pattern if the analyst hadn't been doing some after-hours creeping on the woman's Instagram. Don't blame him much. Smoke show, as I said."

"So Josiah, the deal on the table is trading this name, and likely I hope some corroborating narrative with a juicy set of details, for 150 BattleBox kits; mix as you asked for? And if you pick up a buffalo wing, I may have to end this call."

"Like this one?" Josiah reached off camera and lifted a chicken leg, dripping red sauce, with a hint of blue cheese on its tip. He inhaled the spicy wafterons with a smile.

"I hate you," Jason said. He sniffed and leaned forward. "Have you heard about my new set of responsibilities with the BattleBox SDK team?"

"That you've been..." Josiah glanced at Jason and set the offending piece of chicken back off camera. "How shall I say it, seated? Ah, yes, seated with the project owner role over the three teams and ultimately responsible for the delivery of product. Yes. Quite a promotion for someone with as little major development experience as you have behind your wheels. Congratulations."

Jason was coming to know this snarky little man well enough to note that while the word spoken said one thing, the tone said simply the opposite: I'm sorry to hear. I weep for your sanity.

"I'm hearing you," Jason began his counter offer. "Tell you what, I'll geek to your 150, if you help me with one of my tasks required to fulfill my new role?"

"And what might that task be?"

The offending chicken leg raised back into view and was expertly consumed, college fraternity style. Sauce splashed. Bones dropped off the frame in satisfaction.

"I've on my virtual desk a stack of pre-screened resumes. Around 60 total. Of which I'd like to narrow down the field to only 20. We have 10 slots. Mix of developers and at least one SecOps capable engineer or developer. Could go with a dedicated DevOps or two, if they can also spin the hat around and write or review code."

"And what, exactly, are your criteria?"

"It's well-scoped in the job ads," Jason waved his hand. "You won't have a problem parsing them. Oh, also, if you have any other suggestions for potential candidates, I would be more than happy to entertain them."

"How much time might I have to perform this assessment and potentially offer recommendations? Assuming, of course, that I even remotely consider taking on this task as part of our barter process." Josiah had gotten a strange look on his face somewhere between anticipation and deep concentration.

"Give it a week?" Jason flipped to his dreaded calendar of doom and checked the project timeline against the next sprint. "I'd like to carve out time to let the teams have interviews with candidates next week. We'd be able to offer start dates quickly, laptops delivered as well before a July 1 start date. I'm working with an amazing PM, so that process will fly once we get the right people signed up."

"I'll do it for 250 BattleBoxes. You can pick the hot sauce flavor of the last 100. Either case and battery setup."

Jason acted like he was considering this carefully, but realized he had to set the hook. "You get to select the Security Operations slot, and 200."

"That slot, plus you hire any two others from my list and you have a deal."

"One," Jason countered. "One for sure, and I'll weigh the others and vote for them with the teams. They have final say, though. If your candidate fits; they sit."

"Deal," Josiah agreed, and toasted Jason with his beer. "And you drive a hard bargain, Mr. Richardson."

"I'm going to pour a beer down your shirt when I see you in person, Mr. Ricther. With brotherly affection; of course."

"I will await the dowsing with my breath held and my towel ready to deploy. I hear you," Josiah jolted up from his chair. "Oh, I almost forgot. This won't be in the notes, but going back to this Weatherly critter. He has a saying. Don't all evil people have to have sayings?"

"Like in the movies, when the idiot bad guy goes on a solo rant for no reason instead of just pulling the trigger and ending the hero?"

"That exactly," Josiah nodded, with his next wing raised in emphasis. "This Weatherly guy gets his hands dirty. When he offed the CEO of Ulysses in her untouchable tower in Atlanta, ironically, the same night you were being turned to hamburger, he said a specific phrase. He's said it before; we've extracted it from the last moments of at least three of his assassinations."

"Thank you for the reference. And what, my friend, were those ultimate words?"

"You're not hearing me."

"I'm listening." Jason was momentarily confused as he was actively focused on processing Josiah's words as fast as his brain could follow.

"No, seriously. He said those exact words. *You're not hearing me.*"

Chapter 6

Go Call

The Godmother glared at her clock. Her friends in the business had applied her nickname affectionately. Those she stood against had adopted the moniker in their curses.

The carefully groomed woman in her early 60s plopped down in the old but comfortable leather chair at her antique handmade desk in her polished wood-clad home office. The space was decorated carefully to strike a message into the hearts and minds of those who viewed her camera feed. It was also unfortunately hot and sticky on this day.

Summer afternoons in Boston could get steamy, and this was a slightly above average scorcher. In her youth, the fire departments drove out and cracked open fire hydrants to cool off the masses of kids playing in the streets on days such as this. The time when the cities of her beloved state could absorb the costs of such community service was over. Now, the current generation of elected and appointed officiates, who once spent town funds on cooling down kids with love for their community, argued over every scrap of paper, parcel of land, and sign ordinance.

Godmother opened the call on her calendar after a brief glance at the invite list prepared by one of her many aides.

As a United States Senator, and chair of a rather select behind-the-scenes security committee which involved much of the Joint Chiefs, her role in running things from emergency spending allocations to contracts went all the way to the highest levels. Almost nothing touched the president's desk for his cornflakes briefs each morning without her staff, or often her getting her fingers into the mix. Sometimes it was more than fingers involved in the churn. For this meeting agenda, the contact surface of her involvement was her whole ass.

"Good afternoon," said the Godmother

She paused to grant admission to those stuck in the virtual waiting room.

"Good afternoon, all. Thank you for joining."

Going down the list, she highlighted the first person with their hand icon raised and opened the floor. "Jones, last meeting we requested an update on the situation in Slovakia. Go."

Camera off but microphone hot, the CIA spook lowered his virtual hand in the application.

"Roger. Nothing concrete to report on the region. A team has been deployed to Bratislava. Of note, we have confirmed the Russian government is also aware of the incidents and contracted with Red Protector to investigate. We have confirmation from the Reds that our long-standing mutual assistance agreement is in effect for this contract. As such, we chose to just embed with their team directly."

"Any concerns with that arrangement? They are Russian, after all."

"None expected, Godmother," Jones spoke with confidence. "We worked directly several times with their team, lead on other projects and have a solid relationship with this contractor."

"Drinking buddies? Or just random lab partners?"

"Um," Jones hesitated. "Call it closer to the former, ma'am."

"Thank you, Jones. I'll keep you on the agenda for the next meeting. Anyone else have new business items?"

Seeing no hands raised, she went on.

"Per last meeting, we tabled the launch of an interception operation in the Pacific for the," she consulted a note on her desk. "Looks like the nineteenth time. At that meeting, permission was granted for the RDI led teams involved to move assets to their final stage point and, as able to continue exercises, then hold for our clearance before executing. Any objections against taking a final vote?"

One hand raised. "Yes, General Berger?"

"Not an objection, but a question?"

"Floor is yours."

"I direct this point to Jones and the Agency, but as a reminder across all parties, specifically Homeland; we chose to delay. People needed time and warning to prepare themselves for a potential response. I'd like to ask everyone to weigh those prior discussions and review the current situations of their people. Are we all ready? Have we prepared safe response plans if this explodes?"

"You mean, if we end up causing a nuclear incident in the middle of the world's largest ocean?" The representative from Homeland spoke out of turn.

"The initial concern originated from our analytics teams

based on how our resources had been scattered in the last few months," Jones said. "We've taken, we feel, sufficient mitigating steps, General. But thank you for the callout. I agree with you. We should all carefully consider our current posture in our areas of responsibility."

"Okay then. Let us move on to vote unless there are any other objections or comments?"

Godmother waited thirty seconds and then clicked the snap-in to run a vote in the meeting chat.

As the timer ticked down from 60 seconds, she tapped her fingers, twirled her pen, and took a sip of iced-tea. The results ticked in and made her pause. She clicked her tongue as she had expected another pointless delay.

"I didn't expect a land-slide, folks, but we are officially a go. Ten for and one against. Any other topics to discuss... Hearing none. Please send in agenda items to me for the next meeting in the usual ways. I will remind General Berger that the NSA needs his input on a report they are preparing for our next meeting relating to satellite security. Can you make the time to chat with Sophie soonish?"

"I'd be glad to. I'll compare schedules after."

"Thank you; and thank you all. Out here."

Godmother closed the call and sighed with relief as she pulled out one of her many phones. Her fingers were even and calm as she tapped out a text message to MD with RDI to confirm the "GO" order.

> *Hope your flight to the island went well. It was perfect timing. All systems go for dragon chasing. Go. Go. Go get that ship!*

That done, she fanned herself with a manila folder a few

times. The godmother was about to crack the window for some well-needed breeze given the near overwhelming odor of boiled linseed oil in the stuffy space. One of that burdensome multitude of cell phones she carried daily rang. It was her oldest device, an ancient Android that only worked on one carrier anymore in the states, and then only in spotty locations. However, it had a purpose.

"Go ahead," she said.

After several soft breaths on the other side that bordered on the creepy, a stressed voice spoke. "I know you. I also know you just had a rather important meeting remotely. And then you sent a text. I'd like to know the contents of that text, and the destination."

"If you know me, then you know you likely shouldn't be calling this number. Also you will not get that information from a cold call. What else might you want?"

"What I want is for people to start hearing me," the voice shook with anger.

"Kind of busy here," Godmother sat back in her chair and looked over the electronics on her desk with concern. Many experts had assured her that her setup was secure. Her Cambridge accent went to full power as she continued speaking. "Might be easier for me to consider opening my ears if I knew who was doing the talking. Get me, guy?"

"You're not hearing me!" The voice spoke in a harsh whisper.

A few blocks away on the roof of a walkup apartment building, a medium-sized drone lifted off with a brown paper box grasped under its belly in a pair of arms. The drone gained a small amount of altitude to clear an old TV antenna and tall chimneys on a nearby building, crossed over one major street choked with traffic, scooped down between a pair of tall pine trees which stood guard at a kid's park and then hovered over the godmother's brownstone.

The entire transit from apartment roof to brownstone took only fifteen seconds. Those fifteen seconds were long enough for the Godmother to begin one text, and then switch to enter a part of a more exigent send into her phone to start a trace on the call.

That small stitch of time was not enough to complete either send as the package dropped from the drone into a pile of similarly sized small packages which had been slowly delivered over the morning by air. The impact with the pile initiated a detonation sequence.

Hundreds of deadly shape charges went off like a string of black-cats in a metal pan. The brick walls of the roof edges and the openings in the flat structure for the central drain line funneled the charges downward into Godmother's office.

Between the collapse of the roof, the pressure wave of the explosions, and the resulting hot over flash of fire, the Godmother died instantly. The careful move-set with memorabilia, trophies from her daughter's softball games, and awards from Brain Bowl, theater, concerts, and handmade mother's day cards were consumed in the fury.

From the apartment roof two blocks away, one James Weatherly set down the drone controller, picked up his backpack, and walked towards the fire escape. As a mock salute, he took the last few sips from a bottle of vodka before launching it in the air towards the rising plume of black smoke.

"I will be heard; damn it!"

Chapter 7

A New Toy

"Hey, man!" Collin Duez walked into the farmhouse and hugged his friend Brian carefully. Taking a step back from, he took in the signs of tension on the younger man's face, but also the tanned skin of someone who has been working outside for a season. "I thought I heard an engine."

"Ya," Brian laughed and shook his head. "That would be Molly. She's on the large field today. The one down the hill, near the creek."

"I didn't know you had a tractor."

Something about the look on Brian's face made Collin pause. He raised an eyebrow in question.

"It's," Brian raised his hands and made air-quotes. "Her. Tractor."

"Right..." Collin then realized Brian was serious. "You bought her a tractor?"

"No," Brian moved from air quotes to hands waving in the air and turned to walk into the kitchen.

On the way, he had to fight to kill the random news feed playing from his phone, which kicked back alive when he picked up the device. Collin followed, kicking his sneakers off next to a pair of sawdust covered large boots.

Two beers popped open and were set on the small round table. Collin had enjoyed many of such beers on that table, chatting with Brian and consuming BBQ over their years of working together. He watched how his friend sank down into one of the three chairs, all of which were mismatched and patched, but squeaky clean.

"You sure you should be drinking a beer, Brian?"

"I'm sort of okay having one every once in a while. This is my first one this week."

"Rogue, Dead Guy Ale," Collin sat, took a sip, and nodded. "I approve. I have to ask, since your normal routine for recovering from a pounding on a mission involves, well... a pounding."

"Pounding on the wall, pounding on a case of Scotch plus a shit ton of beers, and then pounding on a punching bag. It's okay, this time's been different."

"Because you had a buddy?" Collin asked softly.

Brian smiled and looked out the window. Seeing that smile from the large man, Collin felt a sudden emotional release and had to sip his beer to keep himself from tearing up. Until Molly had shown up at the Ulysses hanger to hop a plane for Baku and told the giant Brian to suck her toes while getting in his face, Collin hadn't seen his friend smile much in the better part of four years.

Those had been dark years.

Collin took in the kitchen's state. An ancient rack held organized dishes, fresh from a wash. The propane stove was clean as always, sitting next to the small and ancient wood stove which heated the house in winter. The breeze through the open windows smelled of earth and oak.

A corner of the tiny living room area off the kitchen had one of those convertible sit-stand desks with double monitors and a stool. And Brian's 74-inch TV, which Collin had helped install the prior year, still took over what had once been a wall of tiny spoons nestled in little handmade display stands.

"How's the new room? The roof looks good."

Brian nodded, sipped his beer, and then pointed to a nasty gash on his leg.

"Other than slipping once and almost taking my knee cap off with a damn nail, wasn't too hard to frame. We're taking it easy this week before tackling the floor. The new room should be done in a few weeks. Give me a few minutes and then I'll show you."

"And taking a break somehow involves tilling a field?"

"It's a toy to her," Brian shook his head. "Hard part of the last two nights has been getting her in for dinner. I'm serious, man. She's literally using that tractor as a therapy aid. I see her hammer on something at work for a while, and then get frustrated and vanish for a half an hour. Comes back inside, smelling like diesel and earth with a grin on her face, and dives right back in."

"So, you're glad you bought her a tractor, then."

"I didn't buy her a damn tractor," Brian snapped back with a hint of a glare, a pull of beer interrupted.

"Because it's mine. I bought it," Molly stated firmly from the door.

She struggled for a moment to get her second boot off, and then crossed to meet Collin for a hug.

"How are you?"

"I'm fine," Collin said.

He took Molly in briefly before releasing her arms and then watching her walk stiffly to the fridge to pour a glass of water from the dispenser and take a sip.

"My flight back from Taiwan was long, but I needed to get back to my girls for a few days, and the boat won't be in Okinawa for almost two weeks. Nori is playing time games with routes the ship can take. I'll head back next weekend and should arrive with plenty of time to join in on the fun."

"Staying the night with us?" Brian asked.

Collin checked his watch, mentally calculating the drive time from the homestead in the Georgia woods to his home just north of Chattanooga, Tennessee. "Depends on what you're cooking for dinner. While I love your BBQ to death, if dinner is one of your Hell'z Chicken special's, I'm out, brother."

"Before I tell you, I would like to know if you told Meredith you would be home tonight, or tomorrow morning?" Brian asked, pausing only to see how Molly took in the thought of a guest. Since it was technically her place now, he had to remember to consider her comfort.

"It's salmon," Molly said. "More savory than Cajun. I'll air fry up some fresh veggies from the local farms. I hope to have my own vegetables coming in a few months, but got a late start on a garden. You're welcome to stay, Collin. You can take Brian's room."

Brian looked over at Molly's sock-clad feet, and then up at Collin, who was observing the two. The large man with whom Collin had bonded over the years had exhibited a rather profound character trait. He sucked at relationships with women. Now, realizing Collin was sitting in not just his friend's kitchen, but THEIR kitchen was simply strange. Not uncomfortable, but strange.

Collin picked up his phone and tapped out a quick text to Olivia.

"Ask Olivia how she's enjoying all the sunbathing," Molly laughed, knowing exactly who Collin was reporting to with fast fingers.

"And yes, while I wanted to check on you two as well, Olivia demanded that I stop in on my way home."

"To make sure I wasn't bullying Brian around? Or because she wanted to know if we were shacking up?"

Brian growled at Molly. "Can we not start talking about sensitive stuff?"

"He really is... Rather sensitive."

Molly looked over at Collin after carefully setting her glass on the counter.

Collin took in that exchange for a few moments, and then tapped in a second message, nodded his head, and put his phone away, replacing it with the beer.

"Okay, now that I'm off the hook for THAT from the Purple Bunny Rabbit known as Olivia, I will honor Brian's tender skin and leave things as they are. So, seriously, I can't believe the work you guys have done with the addition. But how are you both? Really?"

They spent another hour catching up before Molly tossed the aforementioned batch of veggies in the air fryer and disappeared to take a bath, as she was covered in dust from removing rocks and plowing all day. The men moved outside to the newly covered grill zone and Brian tossed the rested salmon over some charcoal and hickory.

Brian stared off towards the sunset as the smell of wood and sizzling of fish mixed in the cooling air.

"I'm coming back. It'll be many months, I think. But I'm coming back."

"Never doubted it, Brian," Collin nodded. "Lots to do, and lots more to do in the future. I like the RDI guys. They get this world. And you taking a round to a kidney sucks. Not sure how you two came up with this plan to bust your asses so that you heal, but it looks like it's working."

"I'll stick to water, but feel free. I don't mind," Brian nodded over at the next unopened beer bottle on the patio table.

"I have to say, Brian." Collin shook his head and cracked his third beer. "Seriously, I have to point out that you have had a string of girl problems in your years. From that mix-up issue with the barracks bunny, which involved a near discharge, court cases, MPs and an FBI case file. And then picking up an international stalker chick from a dating website... The general tone of your history with women has been a complete shit-show."

Brian snorted.

"How are you not fucking this up?"

"Did Olivia send you to ask me that, Collin?"

"It was a direct order from her," Collin said.

Brian ignored the ear-to-ear grin on Collin's face, checked his watch, and flipped the two large fish fillets.

"There was this moment while we were both hanging out in the waiting room while Jason was literally actually having his guts stitched back together. We were both pouring over some of the hospital documentation about after-care and next-steps and shit. Suddenly, we both realized we hadn't really thought about our own next steps."

"Something in one form the hospital councilor gave us had a section which suggested a concept of one injured vet staying with another injured close by the hospital. Rather than having to go back to their homes for follow-up surgeries and care. There was even a number to call to help find spots or coordinate collaborative stays."

"I guess it makes sense. Most of the people who found themselves in that military hospital usually got there through some rather extraordinary circumstances and were all potentially either void of a support environment or worlds away from such. We helped fill out the forms to secure Jason an apartment with all the wheelchair access he'd need close by. Since he has no family who can help, and really needed to be near Columbus, it made sense for him."

"And you two?"

"I remember seeing Molly pouring over the forms for her discharge, and every time she'd get to the location section, the laptop would come out, and she'd spend half an hour plotting out car rentals, and then checking hospitals near Boston. Eventually, she'd give up, close the laptop and take a nap."

"My place is only a three-hour drive away from Columbus. Close enough to drive back in near Fort Benning, stay the night, and then skip back after a checkup or brief stay for procedures. My plan was simple."

"Jason's down in Columbus, right? Apartment close by the hospital?"

"Yup, there's a whole subdivision of retirement homes which have tons of assisted wings and ADA compliant rooms. It's crazy expensive, but also just a bus ride from the hospital and rehab facilities."

"I guess this matters. How did you talk her into staying with you? Or yourself?"

"For me, it was the food, man. I saw the travel arrangements were spinning Molly into a ball of stress. Her closest family's way down in Southern Florida, her brother. No space to let her crash with a family with a toddler in a one-bedroom cottage on an island. The stress of travel was one thing. Then she opened a tab to sign up for one of those meal services and I just lost it and said she could take my aunt's room for a few weeks until she was in the clear."

"And she just went for it?"

"The girl literally looked at me and blinked a bunch of times, shrugged and said, OK. It didn't even really register for me until we stopped for groceries here in town before heading up the mountain."

Brian drew the fish carefully off onto a plate to rest and sat back down.

"Okay, one last question, and then I promise to let the gratuitous friend grilling session go for the night."

"Go on," Brian chuckled. "Get it over with."

"How long have you been sleeping together? Olivia is going to demand that I let her know when it started."

Brian smiled, knowing that the question was coming.

"That's the funny part, Collin. We haven't. Not joking here. You heard what Molly said. Since the sleeper couch got moved out into the barn to make room for her desk, we only have two beds at the moment."

"Oh." Collin didn't expect that answer. "Oh! Yeah. Really?"

"Too busy," Brian shrugged. "I guess we've just been too busy."

Chapter 8

Busy Work

The absolute crushing stack of paperwork Olivia had been dealing with since Trevor was off escorting their "takeout" order of sneaky munitions on the ship heading to Okinawa while Collin had also taken his week off was the only reason Olivia checked herself out of the training schedule for the day. She instead spent the time madly tapping away on her laptop.

Admin work had deadlines to meet for everything from payroll to drug test validations, quarterly fitness checklists, shipping authorizations, and their latest and least favorite; monthly credit checks. That load had been spread across the senior five people just months before. Now that number was down to a marginally sufficient three thanks to Collin offering to step in to take the fallen Greg Lightfoot's place in the workload.

As locations go for serious work, she had selected her usual spot at the end of the pool in a bikini. Even with shades, the monitor on the laptop was a bit of a challenge to use in the bright equatorial sun. The extra effort was worth it. If she could multitask a tan and fight back against the tide of admin work at the same time? So be it.

Her watch dinged, reminding her she had a half an hour until a meeting. Olivia finished up the last few sections of a required checklist for accepting delivery of a truck full of air tanks from the Tori Station divers supply stores, closed her laptop and then dropped her sunglasses on the little table which had become her desk in the past months.

Taking a few running steps at the pool Olivia dove in, quickly pounded out strokes to the other side and turned over. Her mind now cleared of the drudging busy work by the fifty meter lap, she raised herself up out of the pool and froze. MD was standing about ten feet away, just inside the gate and in the perfect position to witness all of what she had just displayed.

Feeling her face flush, Olivia continued her move to stand and walked over to collect her towel, turning her back as she wrapped it around her torso. Since it was only Cynthia and her normally staying at the smaller of the two houses they had purchased, she had gotten in the habit of, well, going European in her sun experience every morning.

Accidentally exposing herself to anyone else on the crew, she wouldn't have cared for a second. MD; Frances Randal Alexander, however, HIM seeing her with her assets out was completely different and caused her belly to flop over a few times on its way back to level set. Other than the color of her cheeks likely betraying her, and that she didn't fiddle with her top to put it back on, she let nothing slide that the accidental flash had been anything other than an intentional barb on the end of her line.

"How was the flight?" Olivia asked. She juggling the

phone, errant string top, and computer while carefully maintaining towel tension.

MD cleared his throat and took a deep breath. He shuddered, and a glanced out to sea.

"Um... Weather was a bit crappy. Typhoon's going through to the east. The storm won't likely impact us though, unless it does something odd."

"Glad," Olivia nodded and waved MD ahead and back inside. Last thing she was going to do was walk in front of him with her towel not currently capable of covering her rear.

"I know we have a meeting in a few minutes," MD turned into the kitchen and, in a move unlike what she would normally see from the cautious man, he opened the fridge and drew out a Guinness.

MD popped the top on the opener next to the pantry, crashed onto a stool next to the counter, and sipped the dark brew. She knew something was wrong.

"What is it?" Olivia asked.

She set down her laptop and carefully, and slid onto a stool on the opposite side of the center island. Her mind scrolled through the people out in the field at the moment. From Justin Tarbert helping again with something in Somalia to Collin at home with his family. Brian and Molly and Jason, doing their requisite post injury recovery time and Trevor, Fat Al, and Cynthia out on the ship in troubled waters. Who was it this time?

"I know I just got here, but..." MD trailed off and took another sip. "They got the godmother."

"Wait, what?!"

"Ya." MD said.

He continued after a slow shake of his head. "I got the message from her that signaled our long awaited mission GO order and went straight to the airport in Seattle from the consulate in Vancouver. Apparently minutes, maybe even seconds after she sent me the go-ahead text message, some bastard blew up a bomb in her house."

"Dead?"

"Yup. The explosion or the fire also got her dog and her youngster's bearded lizard. Daughter was at college and is okay. Secret Service got her and her sister's family to a safe-house within an hour."

Olivia put her hand on MD's arm. "I'm sorry, Francis. I know you two were close."

"Thanks," MD closed his eyes and shook his head. "This was at a bad time."

"Do you need to head there?"

"A part of me wants to," MD said.

He obviously ran some mental calculus between family and profession. Olivia was one of the few who knew that the godmother was MD's cousin. A second head nod and a sniff confirmed the internal debate was settled.

"No, I'm here in Okinawa until this is done, now that we have the go. Our Director Jun can handle the fallout with the committee back in the states. There's another reason I needed to chat with you immediately."

"I figured there was something up for you to waltz into my layer, beyond the desire to gawk like a teenager."

"I... Um..." MD shook it off, though with a visible hint of difficulty. "We'll deal with that later. This different issue came straight from Berger's channel, through a guy named

Jones. Know him?"

"Of course," Olivia said, then made a face. "Stinky spooky guy. He's not bad. Emski likes his spirit and respects him. That usually means he's worth paying attention to."

"I'm not sure why, but Jones specifically requested, as in made it a personal desire for Jason Richardson to be assigned the investigation into the attack in Boston."

Olivia sat back, panicked for a moment as her towel almost unsettled itself, and raised an eyebrow.

"What? Jason? Why?"

MD raised his hands and kept his eyes up respectfully. "I have no idea. Still thinking through it, I haven't replied yet."

"And you likely need to respond. Fast, I take it." Olivia frowned at her rhetorical observation.

"I know Jason's not walking yet, but it sounds like there's a technological component here, from what little I gathered. Drone involvement, surveillance gear recovered at the scene. Also, there was much of our own encryption gear in her office beyond just a second gen RDI BattleBox. Not to mention the other government issued kit."

Olivia nodded. "Which is reason enough to get someone who has clearance for working with such critical gear at the tip of the spear. I read through some of his work on the KT 4510 investigation with DHS. He's got chops."

"Do you think Brian and Molly can help him?" MD asked that hesitantly. The fact that he had come to her, instead of talking with them directly, had everything to do with the fact that Olivia had been the team lead on their escape from Baku. She knew Brian and Molly best, and also had taken an intense interest in Jason's training since coming onboard with RDI following the escape mission. While the last was to make sure Jason wasn't a threat to Molly at first, she actually liked the kid.

"Think carefully, Francis," Olivia warned, powering up her girl-energy source and giving it the reins. "The last time you put these three together on a task, they ended up being hunted by a battalion of armed soldiers with the support of law enforcement across sixteen counties. Before I can get behind this, you need to convince me, that a repeat is not possible. They all almost died!"

"I know, Olivia." MD gave a sinister glare at the dark glass bottle in his hands. "Charlie company, 3SFG, 4th Battalion. Know them?"

"I know that's a special forces group, but not specifically. And I think I remember that the third group is out of North Carolina. Organized in Operational Detachment Alphas (ODAs), if I recall. Green Berets."

"Correct," MD agreed. "Fort Bragg, but since 2009, at least one company of the 4th BTN has been deployed to Iraq. Charlie was Jason's company when he was enlisted. And since his former company is just rotating off the field, actually just hitting US soil four days ago, we have them as our support."

Olivia bit her lip.

"Active support. Jason gets them. All of them. Full battle rattle flying under the National Guard rules, and anything they need. It's even the same commander whom Jason served with."

"How the hell did that happen?"

"When was the last time in US history a retired Navy had to call a Nine-Line emergency medical evacuation for a retired

Army because his own government fucked up and shot him to shit? People are pissed off."

Olivia nodded and stood. "I'll geek to it, but I want a phone call with the commander. Second part of the question you asked about Brian and Molly?"

The woman stood close to MD and spun her unlocked phone around to show him the texts from Collin.

"Thoughts?" She looked carefully down at MD's face, realized she was closer than her body should be to the man, and padded back on bare feet to let him finish the examination with a bit more space.

"Interesting," MD said, actually flummoxed. "I... Really? Two of the most compatible people I've ever seen. After not one, but two extremely high stress combat encounters where they survive with each other's involvement. Living and working together in the house for months. And ... Really, nothing sooner? How? Their obvious chemistry markers are off the charts?"

"Francis," Olivia glared at him directly. "In a different time or place, with those words coming out of your mouth, I would slap you silly and then drop this towel. Since time is short, call them. You have my blessing to ask. I trust Collin's reading. And even though Jason may get his own boys to help him, don't send him unless he's got Molly and Brian to back him up. Understand?"

"I do," MD glanced at the towel, knowing he was being teased. "Another time?"

"Maybe," Olivia shrugged. "I'm going to go grab that shower now. And the door will be locked. Go make your calls."

"Noted."

MD set his phone on the charging pad on the counter and began fishing in his pockets for his earbuds.

Olivia walked past MD, pausing only to take the towel off after she got behind him, twirl it into a solid coil between her hands and then pop him in the butt just as he'd opened a call.

"Hey!"

Chapter 9

Good Training

"The secret to really good training," Michael Dinkham absently lectured Damion, who was mounted up next to him on a .50 BMG M117 Barrett overlooking a far remote corner of the naval docks at Tori Station, Okinawa. "Is to balance the carrot and the stick. Give too few bites with the stick on the back side, and you get soft. Too many, and the heart falters."

Damion made an adjustment to his optics as he tracked his RDI teammate Randy Wakeman completing a mock "patrol" circuit on the 0-1 deck of an old freighter the Navy had hung onto for training exercises. As the only team member other than Michael on RDI Team A present, Randy got the chance to play the bad guy.

Simulators, blanks and adapters checked and double checked. Corners and buddies called, and safety forms dotted, Michael gave the go.

"Team C; Engage."

The team was temporarily led by Fred Stone, and the boat driver was on loan from the Seals. Collin would likely drive on the mission day, but for now, a stand-in would be fine. A 22 foot RHIB powered by a 300 HP motor came from an idle out of cover and screamed across the short angle of the harbor while accelerating past 50 MPH.

With a kiss of rubber against the hull, three things happened at once. Drones one and two controlled by Hong Nori Lin from his waterproof tablet with their feeds driven through the BattleBox mounted in the RHIB swooped in on Randy and delivered a dummy version of a hybrid taser and tangler in his space. Drones three and four dropped lines over the rail section that had been replaced with the closest example of their target ship they could get their hands on to emulate the actual structure.

Before the team could fly up the boarding ropes on their battery assisted devices similar to the unicycles made popular by YouTubers, a shot rang out from Team N, an all RDI group from their New Mexico office. Their point shooter landed a paintball on Randy Wakeman's chest just as the man cheated and successfully fired a simulated grenade down into the lead boat, which had stuck to the chest rig of the largest target: Ivan Marinov.

Said massive man launched himself off the back of the boat to "save" his team in an impressive flip by a dude weighing in at almost 450 pounds with his gear from a rocking boat.

"Randy, you are toast; all teams play it out."

Ropes burned and boots kissed painted steel. In moments Team N and Team X, the last comprising two all Seal units, slapped three more hulls and boarded at the opposite side with hand dropped grapples and similar boarding aids while Team C cut straight through a man hatch and dropped a few ladders to the engine room. The RDI N team tackled the "lab space" mocked into what was the training vessel's cafeteria, and X moved to bridge and secured.

Total time to secure all the seventeen "mock crew" including Randy Wakeman: twelve minutes and forty seconds. Their fastest time had been under four minutes, but that was only because Randy hadn't cheated, and most of the mock crew they had borrowed from the Navy had been in the entertainment room watching a movie on the first round while unaware of the true purpose of the exercise. After the blistering "loss" of the ship, their petty officer understood the actual game and wised up and sent her sailors out into a more realistic and challenging dispersion.

"Too slow, people. Reset."

"We have one SN who got dinged a bit," the lead from Team X1 called.

"Roger X, status?" Michael frowned. They were playing a proper game here, and Olivia had offered the mock crewman an open bar tab and some extra leave if they would do a good job. Having to go see their medic wasn't in that deal.

"Eh, he's fine," X1 replied. "Just going to send the seaman (SN) off for some stitches. He can take himself. Nothing critical."

"Explain?" Michael now wished his mentor Trevor was here instead of him. He needed to know if they had to change the rules of engagement to limit further injury.

"Call it non-related, R1," X1 lead called back. Michael couldn't remember the officer's name, but the older LT had been fast and careful in all of his actions thus far. The man let a laugh out over the radio as he delivered the explanation. "No reason to terminate under current parameters. We cleared into a bunk with two seamen. One screamed. The second cut himself open as he woke up from a nap and smacked his head on the ceiling over the bunk."

Damion rolled his head away from his scope and laughed. "I've done that a bunch of times myself, Michael."

Shaking his head in relief, Michael opened the mic. "Okay, send the SN home, and make sure he knows he's getting an extra ice cream on us or something. PO Smith? Are you good for a reset, or do your boys need a break?"

"All well here," Petty Officer Smith called over the comms. "Maybe give us an extra five this time? I've never done this sort of thing before. It's fun, but I'm trying to balance hide and seek vs the grab ass. Since most of these sailors haven't been on anything other than a Navy ship; I'm not sure we're all getting the act of emulating a merchant marine crew correctly."

"It's been good training, PO. Good training. Keep trying to punk us within the parameters, and we'll appreciate it."

"Permission to make a small tweak to said parameters, sir?" PO Smith asked.

"While I appreciate the honorifics, PO, I'm not in your chain. Just call me R1."

"R1, permission to request a modification. Perhaps off comms? Don't want any cheating."

Michael grinned, turned to Damion and laughed. "See, now we get into the really good training. This is what I was hoping for."

After a quick verify that the enormous form of Ivan made it back onto a boat, Michael checked the time. Opening comms, Michael did his best to keep his enthusiasm out of his voice.

"PO Smith, give your party an extra five and call my number directly for a chat. It's on the paper with the ROE."

While all the team leads could hear the conversation but not the entire force, Michael wanted to give the solid petty office the chance to make her play.

His phone rang a few moments later as he watched the four boats move back to their respective covers. Randy Wakeman walked forward on the deck to the gear locker at the front of the ship to swap out his "I'm gonna punk you" grenade launcher for something more reasonable.

"Go for R1," Michael answered his phone, channeling Trevor and MD, who had both picked up the habit of answering all calls with that greeting.

"Thank you, sir."

"Again. R1. Or Michael. No need for the sir, Petty Officer."

"Very well," the light and high female voice of PO Smith replied. "One of my guys, he's from a farm, had this idea of..." the young woman giggled briefly, and then choked it down. "Sorry, sir. He had a suggestion of pouring several buckets of floor wax we found on the 0-3 deck down the ladders and in some passageways. Both near engineering and the cafeteria, and into the berthing spaces."

Michael considered for a moment, checked the document Trevor and Elizabeth had drafted on his phone, and then simply laughed. "I may regret this, but PO, that's a go. As when we're doing this for real, we will be in a sea state condition as yet unknown. I'm going with full send. Slippery floors to emulate rolling steel in foul weather checks off a probable box."

"Okay..."

"How many buckets are we talking about here?" Michael asked, suddenly hesitant because of Smith's tone.

"All of them," the woman answered.

"Only thing, PO Smith. Don't do it this reset. Do it the one after. Everyone's expecting mischief this time. Understood?"

"Yes... R1," the woman giggled, grasping the meaning of her mission.

Closing the call, Michael took a few moments himself to grab a snack and sip some water. Back on his scope, Damion who had overheard most of the call, was chuckling as Randy walked back around on his patrol. This time, the token watch patrol was sporting a rather nasty looking shotgun.

"Anyone say anything?" Michael asked Damion, while putting his ears back on.

"Nope."

"Okay," Michael fired up the comms. "Go, team C!"

And fifteen minutes later, they were back in reset mode. "All teams, call that a fast eleven flat. Better. We have a few more before we need to clear the range. Any issues?"

"None here," Stone called from C.

"Clear for go," N said.

"Need one extra to top up a boat, otherwise peachy," came from X2.

Michael let the timer run out after the refuel pause and then clicked a random wait into his phone. All teams reported ready, and all signs were a go.

"Team C; go for insertion!" Michael ordered.

"This may be interesting," Damion mused, watching the RHIB cut out on a line in the harbor.

All went as normal for the initial take down of Randy and the boarding by N and X teams. Then, when team C "cut" down to engineering, the radios began erupting in chaos.

At some point, Michael had put his binoculars down and rolled over on his back to stretch. He may have even cat-napped. Eventually, a very harried Fred Stone announced over the comms. "The boat is secured."

Michael smiled, and looked over at Damion, then checked his watch.

"Well, folks! One hour and five minutes! Wowzah! Anything to report?"

"We... um... all need to clean up," X1 called out, struggling for breath. "No injuries. Somehow. Recommend discontinue training operation. We're gonna need to clean a bunch of gear. Like all of it. And we're gonna need to break out the fire hoses to clear the ladders. This could take a while."

"All teams discontinue operation. RTB for cleanup and retrospective." Michael kept his voice flat until he cut the mic and let the chuckles flow.

"I saw them lifting a ton of plastic buckets up to the 0-4," Damion said as he broke down his weapon system.

"No joke," Michael said. The older man pushed down on his ribs in an effort to set his back into the right position required for an early 50s male who had spent hours watching kids half his age. "It also gave me an idea. Something Jason said once just meshed with what the petty officer had her crew coordinate."

"Do we need more slippy crap?" Damion asked. "With as

much as I saw them pre-stage those buckets around the ship, we're likely lucky no one broke a leg."

"More than that."

Michael pointed to the drones currently stacked up and dropping for a landing into Nori's hands in the distance.

"What was the most epic fail we've had on this? What's the key point we have to get past, to ensure we have a chance in hell of assaulting a defended ship?"

"Always the first line," Damion said. "As it always is with ship assaults, really. And if we lost the initial hit on the patrol, it was usually all over. Then second, getting the crew together in a bunch. Could we fake a fire? That would get people stacked in one or two places."

"Ya," Michael opened up a module on his tablet. "That would work. But I'm also going to see how hard it might be to get one of the initial drone hits to deliver a bunch of super slippery crap to the decks. Maybe even as a pre-strike flyby in the wind for fun in case there are active patrols."

"Otherwise, concerns whether we're ready?"

"Depending on the time, we will do a few more runs once the rest of the people are here," Michael smiled. "I'm happy though."

Chapter 10

Rolling Happy

The last two days were a blur for Jason. He slogged through the time, splitting his attention evenly between finishing the hiring process for the new software engineering slots, delegating on-boarding to others, and splitting out the other product owner duties, and last, on call after call with the 4th SFG's logistics team. While Charlie company's admin staff had been stellar in fielding much of the actual paperwork, everything still had to get his review as their now acting CO.

As he rolled his bag and himself out of the apartment in the muggy Georgia air, and along towards the rental car he had arranged the night before, Jason realized he had made a few mistakes in his planning. He had ordered the rental with hand controls, which he had never taken the time to learn. And second, Jason hadn't quite understood the near impossible task of wheeling heavy luggage while also keeping the chair in a straight line.

Giving up, he let the roller go on its own way down the small ramp. To complete the transit across the parking lot, he alternated between pushing his bag, kicking it, and then throwing it the last few feet to the rear bumper of the small SUV.

Exhausted from the effort, he got the 40 pound roller into the back. And then the button on the key fob to close the rear gate didn't work. A minute of struggle later and he'd stood enough to close the gate, almost catching his fingers.

Back in the saddle, he transitioned to make a bid for the driver's door, which was difficult since the vehicle was parked close to another car rather than in a handicap spot. Swearing, Jason opened the door and cursed.

He'd ordered hand controls, even paid a substantial extra fee for them. This particular rental had no hand controls. Just as Jason was contemplating going with it anyway, even though his feet really didn't respond all that well to input because of nerve and muscle damage at present, an old Toyota sedan pulled in behind.

Jason ignored the sound of the engine at first until it gave a weak little toot from its horn. Jason painfully twisted around in the near-wedged chair to see Brian and Molly waving at him from the sedan. Mixed between embarrassment and warmth at the sight of his friends, he answered with a small wave and backed out of the narrow path and got himself heading towards their car.

"Hi, guys?"

"We got down a little early," Brian shook Jason's hand through the window. "You all set?"

"Actually, would you mind giving me a lift?" Jason sighed and wiped sweat from his face. "I got stiffed on the rental. No gizmos on the column for my hands."

"We'll take your rental the rest of the way. I'll drive."

Molly got out, gave Jason a quick hug, and accepted the keys.

Jason wheeled himself out of the way and Brian parked his car off in a clear area with plenty of room for Molly to move the rental nearby for gear transfer and give Jason room to pick a seat. Not taking help, Jason completed the maneuver of leg transfer, butt slide, and then wheel chair disassembly he'd been schooled on in rehab a hundred times. It didn't mean the maneuver was easy, but it beat the potential shame of being picked up like a little kid.

"Brian filled me in on most of the broad details, Jason," Molly started, pulling onto the highway for the brief drive to Fort Benning. "I'm missing important things, though. Like why I had to give my physical dimensions. Or..."

"We're going to space," Jason joked. "Had to fit you for a suit."

Molly glared over at Jason, then caught Brian trying to hide a laugh in the back seat.

Waving his hands. "Sorry, don't worry. Nothing other than a 35,000 ft puddle jump up to Boston in a C-130. Since we're going official US Government on this, I figured setting up everyone with US Army uniforms was the right play. Fewer questions, both from the troops we will travel with, and the other agencies who are getting their toes stepped on."

"How does that work?"

"Happens all the time out in the field, Molly. Contractors get issued ACUs, basic uniforms, but with no ranks or unit patches while in combat theaters. We're heading for field work, but on-base admin postings often follow dress codes with ribbon racks. There's a whole standard manual for the practice. Little things, mostly details like Brian here, can't wear any previous campaign patches, or units he was a part of. There are some exceptions to that for some long-term detachments, but you two are short term. Also, certain combat medals can be worn. Purple hearts, for example, if in Blues."

"Even though Jason here left as an O-1, he can't put on his former rank or his Rangers or Special Forces tabs. No scrolls either. And I can't put on my cutlass and pistol."

"Actually," Jason looked out the window, and then back. "In my case, I have been hit with a title 32."

Molly shook her head at the jargon. "Huh?"

"It means someone way up the chain gave him a temporary activation," Brian explained, and then groaned. "Oh, no. Here comes the big head! What did they bring you in as?"

After a bit of hesitation, Jason gave in. "Captain. Sorry, Brian."

The man made a sound somewhere between a snort and an aborted chuckle. "Since I'm no longer enlisted, I don't have to put up with your BS. Doesn't bother me."

"We're getting most of a full company of special forces from 3SFG, Charlie Company. Which is likely why they bumped me up. While I had sort of finished OCS, I got discharged before the paperwork went through. I had been acting LT technically during an active deployment previously and that counts or something. Long story."

"Do I have to wear the uniform?" Molly asked quietly, her hands gripping the steering wheel tighter than necessary.

"I'd suggest it," Jason said. "A part of this errand, or so I was coached, is a show of force. The whole point of a uniform is to focus on such forces."

"I'll consider it," Molly sniffed, then took a shaky breath.

"You okay there, Molly?" Brian asked.

Molly wiped a tear away and nodded after a quick check of her composure. "Okay. I, just..."

"She has multiple letters from every branch of service in a shoe box," Brian spoke softly for Jason's benefit. "All denying her enlistment because of medical reasons. Some jackass doctor in Baku tried to shit-can her when we got there with Ulysses this spring."

"That explains it, I guess," Jason connected the dots. "I'd just assumed you didn't want to serve. What was their issue? Or should I not know?"

"If I don't take a pill; I die," Molly answered. A little shrug followed the admission.

"Thyroid issue," Brian explained. "It's well handled. Kind of stupid for the branches to keep some of their requirements, but I view it like the vision issues in the past. Like tons of fantastic people have been denied the right to serve this country over their eyesight."

"Or," Jason snorted. "They just cheated. I read a book about this dude, Willis Lee. This guy in 1920 won 5 Olympic gold medals for sharpshooting, but was denied by the Navy for a promotion due to bad eyesight the next week! Five medals!"

"Seems a bit shortsighted of them." Brian passed up a bottle of water from his pack to Molly, lid off.

"Anyway, I get it, I think," Jason weighed his next words carefully, ignoring the pun from Brian. "You don't have to put on a uniform if you don't want to, Molly. If you wish to be our civilian token mascot, I won't stand in the way."

"Nah, I understand." She dropped the bottle into the cup holder, a third of it gone. "A uniform front is a uniform front. Sorry, guys, I just never thought I'd be a part of something like this. Caught me by surprise."

"She also has a shoebox of all the crayons she keeps earning," Brian added.

"They make great snacks," Molly quipped, cracking a smile.

"I'll try to keep the briefing suitable for 2-year-olds," Jason opened up his phone and checked the calendar while deftly intercepting the halfheartedly cast slap from Molly with his left hand. "We're a little early. There's a Mexican restaurant near the base. Want to meet with the company sergeant manager and a few leads beforehand for a late lunch?"

"I can get behind that," Brian said. "We were going to stop for a burger after checking on you until we got distracted by your vehicular issue. Mexican sounds good though. Not much around my way. Sometimes pleasant distractions are welcome if they come with a free lunch."

"I hear you," Jason nodded. "I've been more than a little ..." Sitting up straight, Jason quickly flipped to his secure emails and scrolled through the last few days. "That little bastard!"

"Everything okay?"

"Probably, Molly. Just ... Oh, shit. I think in my state of juggling fires I messed up something," Jason frantically scrolled through a document. "Yea. I got duped."

"Serious?" Brian reflexively checked his notifications to see if something happened.

"Maybe not, but I don't like being duped; or used," Jason relaxed back and sighed.

"The damage, or I don't know, karma deliverance or something, has already been done. Remember how I was complaining in our chats about being bumped up to own the BattleBox SDK product delivery? Well, that also meant we needed more people. I naively thought I could go toe to toe with a little guy with a foot fetish on a barter. Josiah Richter had contacts I didn't, and we have made a few exchanges of information for hardware. Since I had an enormous stack of resumes and I was too distracted to take the time to review them myself, I tried to get him to help."

"So, does this impact our current investigation?" Brian queried slowly, thinking through the general nature of its scope.

Jason laughed and pocketed his phone.

"Not directly. I had offered Josiah the chance to add some resumes to the stack and then asked for his help to pick the top candidates or weed out bad ones. Something about the Willis Lee story reminded me I hadn't actually compared his list to our original to see if, for example, I was being cheated. He didn't add ANY candidates, even though I'd offered to hire a few off his recommended list to keep him engaged."

"That would mean..." Molly came to the same conclusion with a nod.

"That he had already put all of his people in the pile. All likely CIA resources or contractors of some sort in his pocket had their applications in the stack. And all before I brought up the subject."

"Sneaky," Brian laughed.

"I'll write up a note to Trevor and Olivia and see if they have anything to say. Honestly, I wanted a few of his people to be on the project; just not an unknown number, since we might have hired all of his selections."

"Is this it?" Molly asked, having turned off the major road towards Fort Benning and in sight of a huge sombrero over a cowboy boot for a sign. "Al Gave?"

"Yup." Jason sent a text to the circle of leads he had been in the last few days. "ODA Squad leads are leaving the base now. Should meet us in ten."

Chapter 11

Ten Minutes

"All it takes," Michael tapped a stick on the large dry-erase board at the front of one of the briefing rooms in one of Tori Station's sensitive compartmented information facilities (SCIF). "All it takes, folks, is ten minutes. Our basic process and planning is sound. But now is where the actual work begins. Olivia?"

"Thank you, Michael," Olivia stood and immediately looked over to the newcomer, a plain and stout woman in Navy uniform sitting basically at attention.

"We've added Petty Officer Smith to this final briefing for a few reasons. First, her efforts to lead her men to kick your asses into shape was enough to earn her a seat at the table. And second, she'll be joining our crew in support on the ship since she won the drone piloting competition. While we have intentionally kept this operation small, taking in excellent help when it crosses our path is the way RDI does battle."

"When I say the last briefing, I mean that here on base, we are done. To add to that intentional size restriction, most of you do not know the full nature of our mission. Because of a storm, our timeline has shortened by three days. Our support ship will be here late tonight. After refueling and loading, we expect to leave port around 0800 and begin our transit to our objective."

A few grumblings rippled through the room, and Olivia addressed that by holding up a hand.

"You're going to hate this more. No one leaves. Off mission contact on or off base is locked out for all of you. Charters have been hired to take us to ... somewhere ... around 0400 to begin a clandestine transfer to sea. We all sleep in the SCIF tonight."

"Also, we are also implementing a play from the Agency's book and restricting all internet, cellular, and smoke signals as we transit. As of this moment, your asses are mine. And once you hear what my friend is about to tell you, I believe you will understand our chosen security posture. Words matter. Phrases kill. Conversations destroy. Don't have any outside unless ordered to engage. I know different units have different practices. Each of you has access to a networked drive inside the facility and you are welcome to store any last call sort of messages or notes or instructions on that resource."

"Next up is Collin Duez. While he was originally going to drive Team C's boat, the current loaner, Williams, is going to keep his coxswain slot. We decided Collin would be needed onboard more than behind a wheel. Collin is here with us for a very important reason, and having him a part of the boarding party will be pivotal. While a retired Navy SWCC by origin of service, Collin also taught a series of EOD and NCB courses for the Army. That nuclear, chemical and biological specialty is the key here. Listen to what he has to say. If he runs, you run faster. If he ducks, you make yourself small. If he prays, you pray harder. Understood?"

Nods around the room answered her, and Olivia passed the floor off to Collin. His hair and button-down shirt were damp from an obvious dash from a car through the afternoon tropic shower. Inserting a stick onto the laptop on the podium, he kicked up a presentation.

"Good day, all," Collin started, and checked his watch. "I thought I'd have a bit more time, too, before comms lockout. My daughter is right about now pitching for a state championship softball game, and I will not know how it went for days."

After a few chuckles of understanding, Collin continued.

"First; our ride," Collin flipped to a few pictures of the 250 foot long buoy tender, which he had loaded in Taiwan with Trevor and Cynthia. "The *Sandy Stewart* is small and will be cramped with our teams. The berthing compartments are straight out of a navy sub, so bring tape and cardboard to avoid cutting your heads."

"*Stewart's* a good ship with a stout and vetted crew. They have lots of experience doing these sorts of operations along with moving heavy things and tending expensive pieces of equipment in the deep. I've been told the food is good, but the gym sucks. However, since this is the tropics, and the season for cyclonic action is upon us, she will struggle if we are in a snotty condition. Plan accordingly with your packing, stowing and preparation. If you expect to need seasickness meds or any refills, put in the request to Michael and he will forward it to the base hospital."

"Now that you know the ride, let's go to the target," the

screen flipped to a track out in the ocean east of them. "For the last three months, we have been observing the movements of this specific ship. I won't give the name. Target A has been confirmed at significant loss of life, limb, and liberties to be a mobile fabrication shop which is producing viable nuclear warheads for direct sale in the dark markets."

The screen flipped to show a clone of a W82 mortar in the back of a white pickup truck.

"Many of these 80 pound warheads have been produced. We had the experience of intercepting one as it was being launched. Some friends of ours destroyed five more. The total number produced of this type is only an estimate, as is the potential stockpile of such warheads on the target ship. Also, we are unaware yet whether other types of munitions have been constructed in this lab. And now you know why we canceled your pre-deployment hangover. This could suck, and we all need to be focused. We also must let no one know we're stalking down this ship."

"Now, a little about what we DO know these guys can make. The W82 as a packaged munition is a dual mode round, ideally coupled with an airburst delivery system. In light mode, it's equivalent to a 500 ton pop. No sprinkles. Think of it as a suitcase sized object capable of taking out a building, breaching a dam, or turning a large ship into a reef."

"How many people took the NCB course in Louisiana?"

A few hands raised. Collin pointed to a short guy with enormous arms and black wavy hair from Team X.

"Okay, chief, what are the sprinkles I referred to?"

"Gamma shits!"

"Correct." Collin advanced the slide to show two dispersion patterns, on two rows. "The top row shows a ground detonation in the two modes. The bottom, an ideal airburst height at a thousand feet up to get in the pressure envelope of doom. Left column; non-boosted mode. Right column; add the sprinkles. Sprinkles are bad."

"Keep this in mind. If something happens which results in a detonation, which of the two modes we deal with will directly influence your chances of survival and choices you may have to make to survive."

"If a non-boosted initiation happens and you're inside a hull, get low and inboard. Ladders internal in the ship's core are your best bet. If you're outside and can't get in and down, go for the water and swim down as far as you can. You might get the trots for a week, since the anti-rad meds ensure it even if the initial radiation doesn't mess up your gut flora, but your chances are GOOD if you can go deep."

"Now, the unfortunate part is, in boosted mode, those 'gamma shits' go right through almost everything. These will affect your electronics if they are on, and might mess up some things if they aren't. Distance is the only actual solution. Remember this chart. Consider 2 miles a minimum safe range, with vector away from the fallout. Questions thus far?"

"Do we get those little badge thingies?" Team X's chief petty officer asked.

"Dosimeters," Collin said.

He unzipped his roller bag and pulled out his plate carrier, patting his radio.

"You already have them. All our comms systems have them integrated. We also get that data, so if any soldier is exposed and in the mesh range of anyone else, the network will know of your situation."

"Heartwarming," the NCO leaned back in his chair.

"Here's a little good news." Collin drew a small pelican case out of the same bag, dropped it on a table and then pulled out a cylindrical device with some wires. "This initiator is dead, but I'll pass it around. Take a good look at it. Without something like this device, those W82 nukes that are being fabricated are, as a friend said best, nothing more than spicy doorstops."

"Without an initiation device, of which this is a recent but effective example, there is almost no way to make these warheads go off on their own. They were engineered to be fired out of a frigging 155mm howitzer. One of these little nukes can be shot with a max tube charge, fly 30 kilometers, and impact a stone escarpment and they will NOT go nuclear unless triggered."

"We also know this lab wasn't in the business..." Collin delivered air quotes around the word. "Of making initiators. Others are or were. We can not discount the chance that one or more active nuclear devices may be present on that ship. We know, with high certainty, that several nuclear warheads ARE on that ship, and that there is raw material on board to facilitate that manufacture. Questions thus far?"

Seeing nothing but stern faces, Collin waved over to Olivia.

"Order of mission remains. Take that ten minutes you all have been working on so hard and apply it to securing the crew. Since we have changed our plans slightly, thanks to the epic work by the Navy seamen we were practicing against, we will also shuffle around boat orders and teams slightly. There are two more details to add, though."

"First, we have a care package on our ride waiting for us. We will spread some extra mutations, including C4, scuttle charges and thrombotic rockets among the teams, into the hands of those trained. Collin will work with you all on the way out to get that gear distributed and have some fallback plans in place. We are willing to just flat-out destroy the ship, but the intelligence onboard is of extreme importance. Each boat team will have the ability and the authority and most importantly... I can't say this lightly, the responsibility for a method of sinking that ship. If we can not execute our plans, that ship goes to the bottom."

"And last," Olivia grinned. "When we arrive and start our boarding, the target vessel will be a little distracted. I can't go into details, but we will have an advantage."

"Questions?"

"How do I get out of this chickenshit outfit?" MD smirked at her.

"*You secure that, Hudson!*" Olivia quoted back, channeling Sergeant Apone's voice from *Aliens* and fighting a grin. "No worries. We don't expect this to be a bug hunt. No Xenomorphs, or face huggers. Seriously, though. MD. Was there anything we left out?"

"Only one thing comes to mind," MD frowned. "There is nothing I hate more than losing people. Talk with your leads and within your team once we are at sea about how far you wish to go. While the intelligence we may gather is, as Olivia stated, of extreme importance, I'd ask for you all to not gamble your lives on that. We get what we can, get out, and blow the boat. Don't die for a piece of data which we don't even know will help protect our country."

The room was rather silent for a few moments as the words settled in. And then the power went out.

Chapter 12

Recovery

Within an hour of landing the C-130 at Fort Devens, Massachusetts, Charlie Company's three Special Forces ODA teams, a short squad of company admin staff, and two RDI contractors had mounted up on the idling national guard equipment and rolled off towards Boston. Their haul from the motor pool via requisition form included four MRAP-Maxxpros, assigned to ODA 3432 and 3435, and twelve Humvees, with a mixture of armor, arms and configurations split across the remaining double-sized ODA 3430.

Molly had been the first to get her vehicle turned around from the random snarky snarl of parking Tetris that the national guard crew had left for them. As the first at the gate, and also since Molly knew the route to the street of their target location without a GPS, she had led the convoy onto MA-2.

"Are you sure you know the way?" the company sergeant, Anthony Timmons, asked from the passenger seat, scrolling on his phone.

Jason had reminded Molly that while he was "sort of"

in charge as the captain, a company was essentially run by its most senior sergeant. While Jason may give orders, the responsibility for executing those orders was in the hands of the E-8 senior NCO in her passenger seat.

"Keep on Route 2, turn right at Whole Foods on Auburn, and then snake past Tufts until we get to the playground on Winchester, and then a left on Newbern."

"That's not what Bing says," Timmons frowned and showed her his phone.

She shook her head. "It's 0700, trust me, you do NOT want us on I-495 in an hour. It's a parking lot all the way past to Lexington from then until half past 0900 on a good day."

"Okay," Timmons looked back at Brian, who was in the back seat, as if asking if the man could help. The large man's expression was rather blank, but he had his camera out and dropped his phone back down after getting no verbal response. "Woman driver it is."

A few moments later, Brian's camera sneaked through the pass between the front seats and he snapped a picture of Molly. She was outfitted in standard issue basic combat uniform, flag on arm, kit ready for battle, helmet with a jauntily dangling strap. Then he clicked another. She noticed and turned with a half smile and waved him back.

"Hey! Stop!"

"Can I get another one with you holding a Crayon in your mouth or something?" Brian asked. "For Collin, of course. Scrapbooking is his thing."

"Brian..." Molly warned, checking her mirrors and counting to make sure the last vehicle stuck with her instead of turning onto I-495. "These things really are gutless trucks."

Timmons picked up on the comment. "You sure you got it? Never driven a Humvee before?"

"There was a reason we put her in the lead truck when we were getting the US Ambassador out of Baku, Timmons," Brian spoke calmly from the back seat. "And it wasn't because we enjoyed watching her ass."

"But you do?" asked. "Don't you?"

"Of course!"

"I will smack you," Molly huffed, and turned to Timmons. "Either of you."

With a smile on his face, Timmons shook his head and held his hands up in surrender. Brian passed up a phone with a picture of a white Toyota HiLux, dinged up, peppered with hundreds of bullet holes, and with dark fluid covering the vinyl seats.

"That was some swiss cheese," Timmons grunted and passed the phone back. "Was that her work?"

"And some of her blood," Brian added.

"Okay, I'm with it," Timmons checked a roster under a flap on his vest for a moment and then radioed. "Tail End Charlie, this is Lead 1. Spacing and pacing OK?"

"Roger, lead."

"What did you show him?" Molly asked. She double checked her speed and marking the needle as close to 50 MPH as the shuddering wide vehicle seemed to want to go.

"One of Trevor's snapshots of your poor abused truck in Baku," Brian answered. "Let's not do that again."

"Hey, that little truck stopped a 2kt nuke from taking out a major oil refinery..." Molly looked over at Timmons. "Oops.

You didn't hear that."

"Hear what?" Timmons knowingly blanked the comment from his mind. "Did you fart or something, Brian?"

"Oh, I hope not!" Molly reached forward and cracked the window vent. "And never give that man cheese!"

Brian snickered, thought for a moment about whether he could squeeze out a fart to complete the circle, but didn't have enough wind stored up.

Other than a few snarls near Tufts University, the convoy arrived at the neighborhood of their target location in just over an hour.

"3432-A, tail two and four; break south one block and set up a perimeter. 3432-B, tail one and three; break north for same. Lead 1, pull right up to the police line and wait. Lead 2, 3, 3434-B fan out and block the street in stagger. Rest fall in on lead 1," Jason concluded the order, and Timmons immediately began barking out brief call and answer verifications to each squad with cover assignments: left, right, forward, back, up.

As ordered, Molly made the turn on Newbern Street, instantly coming into view of a string of police cars, a fire truck and a large excavator on a low-boy cluttering the cramped space. Blocking it off would take little more than a bit of an angle for any of their vehicles.

Nearing the police tape, Molly slowed with a squeak of brakes and looked at the rubble on the left. Not much remained of the brownstone. Steam still rose from a portion of the back wall on the second story. Char coated the crumbling bricks. A chimney, mostly intact, pointed at the sky like a giant middle finger.

"That's what we have to sift through?" Timmons said. He frowned at the pile of debris, took in the surrounding old but maintained houses and the uneven roof lines. Most of the near units had broken windows, some taped, some covered with plastic or wood.

On the dismount, Brian ran back to Lead 4 and helped Jason by tossing the assembled wheelchair next to the door. He did not give the man help in getting out, as that would have hurt his entrance.

Timmons and Molly, both sporting M4s in full rattle, flanked Jason as he moved to the tape line. The uniformed police officer on the line raised it for them without a word. The lead party went through, followed by several of the 3430 ODA.

"There was a reason I asked for the '30 guys," Jason said to Timmons softly. "This is an engineering problem. And I wanted people who know how to un-engineer something."

"I heard the Army was sending someone," a tall man in a suit spoke in a fluster, walking their way from a conversation with a man in a fire department polo shirt. "Not an entire platoon!"

"We would be them." Jason rolled close and extended a hand. "Captain Richardson, Charlie Company."

"Detective Hobbs," the man started in to complete the shake and then did a double take with his hand halfway out as his eyes scanned over Molly. "Turner?"

"Oh," Molly involuntarily took a half step backwards. "Crap."

"You two know each other?" Jason looked over at Molly, who had regained her composure before he could process her expression.

"Molly Turner is probably a little mad at me still for keeping her locked to a bed for a few hours," Hobbs said. "Nothing personal."

"None taken, Detective Hobbs," she glanced over at Brian to make sure the man tried nothing. "What are you doing all this way from Framingham?"

"I was transferring to Cambridge a long time back. Your brief scuffle in Framingham was one of my last cases there. Our daughter goes to school out this way. Less of a drive to babysit my granddaughter."

"Reunion aside," Jason eyed the fire department guy who had turned to watch them while he continued a conversation with a group of three with city utilities shirts. "Who do we get to give us permission to excavate the wreckage? Fire marshal and city, I'm assuming? And what do you have about the bad guy's location?"

"First one is going to be touchy," Hobbs started.

"I have a very heavy hand here," Jason let a hint of cold sneak in. "And I am willing to issue a slap. Just point me to the person."

"The second I can help with," Hobbs pulled out his notebook, slowly scratched out Jason's name and rank on a new page, paused again to count the number of people and vehicles, and then barely resumed speaking before Jason lost his patience. "Uni's canvas pointed us to a group of apartment buildings four blocks over. Some kids playing hooky said they heard buzzing and saw packages flying around. They thought it was some sort of Amazon delivery program or something."

"Packages?"

"Correct," Hobbs nodded. "Lots of them. Maybe shoebox

in size? Large shoebox? Just cardboard boxes."

"An exact address, or approximate?" Jason asked.

"Could be one of three, but one local is pretty sure it's this one," Hobbs scratched out the address and tore off a sheet and passed it to Molly. "The other two are owned, not rented. All have been stable for decades, generations even. The middle one, though, has a vacant apartment on top, isn't in the best condition, and has been known to the local PD to be a home for transients."

"And..."

"And once we got the word, after the canvas, we have been working in a reduced mode; observe, record and report only. I may have put someone out to watch the house for any activity, but I would tell you if that source saw anything."

Molly raised an eyebrow and paused from examining the satellite images of the address. "Hobbs? Really, mister straight shooter? I thought more of you, sir."

Holding up his hands in surrender, Hobbs ducked a little. "I slipped a kid a $20 to keep his eyes up. That's all, nothing hinky. I just don't want the kid involved. He has enough problems. Having the Army National Guard, Homeland, FBI crawling in his face won't help him any."

"Molly, can you take Timmons and some boys and go check out that address? I believe I'm about to have a rather nasty conversation with some people and would rather save your ears."

"You, Jason?" Molly shook her head. "I didn't even know you could curse. I got it, and the line of sight to that address is good from the maps. It would be an ideal spot to do some drone operations."

"How many packages?" Brian scratched his chin and looked critically at the fallen structure, wishing he had Collin along. The EOD specialist would have been able to do the math in his head for what a destruction would need.

Hobbs shrugged. "Lots. Kids weren't sure. Maybe fifty or more."

"That could do it," Timmons said. "That number could have held a few hundred pounds of shaped charges. Add in some incendiary explosives? Not a terrible concept. Death by delivery service."

"Timmons, who is the LT for 3430? I only remember corporal, er, now Sergeant Lee."

"It's Davis. First LT."

"LT Davis, come up front to the fire truck, please?" Jason called over the radio and shooed Molly away. "Go on, take one of the MRAPS and two Humvees."

Brian almost moved to follow and then made his choice to stay near Jason. Molly and Brian exchanged a brief glance, and she nodded for him to stay on the captain.

Not noticing the exchange, Jason wheeled over to the four men discussing utilities and waited with his fingers folded in his lap for any of them to realize he was being courteous, or for a break in the conversation to happen.

Since it was a rather stiff argument about whether water or natural gas would be disconnected first, and both sides kept getting complaints back from the power guy about why he had to leave a square block offline when he could be on his way to breakfast in ten minutes if they would shut up and let him finish... Jason felt his patience tick onto its last health bar and cleared his throat.

"Gentleman," Jason spoke. "I'm Captain Richardson, and I'm here to help."

While the conversation paused at the interjection, the gas guy looked like he was about to start back up, and then fully noticed the uniformed man with kit and a rifle extending out of the back of the wheelchair in a holster like those used in old westerns. It took some effort, but the man caught his next words.

"Thank you," Jason continued. "As I began, we are here to help with the situation at the request of the Governor. We just spoke with Detective Hobbs, and will begin working with his people to investigate the root cause. We are required to dismantle the remains of the residence. There are several items we need to secure in the structure while we begin analysis to identify the person or persons responsible for this attack."

"For all we know," water complained. "This was just a gas leak."

"That," Jason pointed at the demolished building, and then turned to the man with the red logo on the shirt. Red for spicy dirt. "That was NOT a gas leak. You're the electrical point of contact?"

"Yes, sir," the man said.

"I don't like spicy dirt. And people are going to need their microwaves and air conditioners and car chargers going. What do you need to do?" Jason held up a hand to cut off the gas man from continuing.

"Simple. Just need to do a pole disconnect, then we can drop the lines that had been attached to the weather head and render the structure safe. It will take longer to bring my crew up the street and set up for the lift than the actual work. Ten minutes. Tops once we get moved in."

"Do it," Jason ordered.

Gas complained. "No! We need to get in first and make sure our lines are secure. Less chance of secondary explosions."

Jason looked over at the building, sniffed the air, and then looked up at the power pole a hundred feet away. "How long would that take?"

"Couple of hours, at least. We have a crew out on another task and will need them here before we can get started."

"We have an excavator right down the road," Jason thumbed over his shoulder.

"It has to be our crew." Gas shook his head. "We have all the equipment to not break a line."

Jason looked over at the fire department chief, who was trying to hide his laughter. "I'm going to call BS on that. Chief, any concerns about electrical getting their clear on?"

"None, son," the silver-haired tall guy crossed his arms and looked over at Gas as if daring him to complain more.

"Go now," Jason keyed up his mic. "Company; assist as needed. Enable the local electrical crew to move up resources."

"Okay, Water," Jason ignored the gas guy. "What do you need?"

"Unfortunately, with a building this old, the cut-off is in the basement."

Jason followed the glance over to the remains of the front porch and then they both looked back at each other. "Yeah. I have a feeling that's going to take a while."

Lieutenant Davis, from 3430, had walked up prior and had been carefully listening along. "Does your crew have any OPAPs on the truck?"

"Maybe one or two," seeing where Davis had gone with the line of question, water nodded. "We may have one the right size for the main line to the house, but we also have boxes of valves we could install with a good clean cut. We'd need someone to excavate the pipe for us, though."

"Do you have the gear to tell us where it is?" Jason asked, checking over his shoulder at Davis.

"Of course."

"Davis, can you get the excavator off the truck and help our water guy cap his pipe?"

"Gladly, sir," Davis nodded over at Water.

"Go on, then," Jason opened comms. "Company; also clearing a water crew. LT Davis will work with them to sort an issue. Assist as can."

"This is not how this is supposed to work," Gas complained.

Jason looked over at the fire chief. "Since I don't know how many people on the block are currently without the ability to cook their breakfast sausage because of the gas being off, and it's not the dead of winter, help me out here? What would you suggest?"

The man looked up and down the street and counted in his mind. "Eh, punt it. Leave it off. Ain't but three houses on this street who have meters, and the other two can deal for the day."

"Thus, gas is punted. If we see that utility line, we will cap it. Don't worry, I'll make sure my boys are nice. Check back with us tomorrow morning."

Gas glowered at Jason, looked over at the fire chief, threw up his hands, and moved off to his pickup truck to take a slug of his coffee and pout.

Jason sighed and looked up at the chief. "Any chance you can leave us one of your crews today. I'd like to keep one of your teams and trucks handy. Feel free and switch them out on a rotation."

"This was a bomb," the chief shook his head. "And ya, we'll keep guys with you. I'll make sure the local station sends the more experienced. Since you seem to know how to run a scene, I can grant you that courtesy."

"I'll get there, but for now, I just know how to read people at this point in my life," Jason sighed, and his left leg decided to suddenly cramp up and then spasm.

Detective Hobbs, who had been listening and trying to not get in the middle of a pissing match, watched as Jason leaned forward, made a fist with his right hand, and jabbed his pointed thumb into his left calf. When the tremor stopped, Jason leaned back and looked up.

"That looked like a bad one," Hobbs said, his voice very low. "Sorry, I was just coming over to see what I could do."

Jason looked up at the chief and nodded. "Thanks, sir. Make sure and let your crew know we will order pizzas or Italian subs for lunch. Or maybe both."

"Take care, son," with a wave, the chief walked ahead on the road, hopped in his truck, and drove off.

The large excavator fired up halfway down the block behind them and the boom truck from the electrical crew slalomed through the staggered line of army vehicles.

"I've seen that reaction in paraplegics," Hobbs said.

He realized his hand was on the grip of Jason's chair, removed it, and then continued.

"But most of them I've worked with don't have to grind enamel off their teeth to hide the pain. Since they don't feel it."

"Blessing, and a curse; I was told," Jason said.

He regarded Hobbs and then decided he liked the man's careful awareness. He had not noticed the near instinctive desire to help Jason in his moment of pain. "Nerves are a bit scrambled. Instead of feeling nothing below the waist, I sort of randomly feel, well, like everything all at once. Only issue is it manifests as you just saw: pain."

"What do you need me to do, Captain?"

"Please keep the units you have here on site. We may need them to deal with traffic. Also," Jason reached into a pouch in his carrier and drew out a notepad. He tore off a page and passed it to Hobbs. "Can you send a message out to the locals that we will stand up the examination portion of this investigation at this location?"

Jason watched the excavator driven by Davis himself pause for a Humvee to pull aside.

"This is a warehouse," Hobbs noted and checked his phone. "Just over in Jamaica Plain?"

"Ya, and that's where we are taking all of this." Jason waved his hands around in a circle.

"And not to some secret undisclosed government facility," Hobbs said, and then instantly regretted it at the sniff from Jason.

"While I served in the Army, Detective, my current rank

and status are temporary due to the nature of this situation and mission. That's not general knowledge, Hobbs, and please don't put it in your little notebook. Issue is, this isn't the only fire going on; but it's a ball which Molly, Brian, and I can field. Marginally, in my case, as you noticed. However, we will field this ball."

"I can respect that honesty," Hobbs said. "Molly is a damn good girl. When I watched that tape of her being ambushed in her car, I almost couldn't believe it was real."

"Spoken like a true father of a daughter."

Jason frowned and willed his leg to stop its second attempt at a show. He looked over his shoulder and realized he needed to move, as not only the excavator was heading towards his general location, but it was being followed by a line of seven dump trucks they had rented for the process.

"Can you pass me your card? So I can directly hit your phone?"

Hobbs did so and then realized he needed to move his car out of the line of trucks before he got boxed in. He paused after one step away and turned back.

"Jason, this has nothing to do with anything other than my history and your condition. But, before you leave Mass, I'd suggest you see an acupuncturist down in Newton. It's less than an hour south of here. I just... Can't find the words. But consider it?"

Hobbs scribbled a name and number on the back of his card before handing it over.

Jason grasped Hobbs's hand. "Thank you for taking care of Molly."

"I.." Hobbs stuttered. "I still feel like I fucked that up."

"Nah," Jason shook his head. "Dude. You did everything right and within the law from what I saw. We needed that. MOLLY needed that at that moment; even if it was inconvenient. Also, now that I got your card. I'm going to start two video conference calls a day on this, and you're getting an invitation!"

"Yay?" Hobbs winced slightly and turned to jog off to his car to remove it from the clogged street.

"Yay," Brian spoke over Jason's shoulder in a deadpan tone.

"Yaw!" Three other army Jason hadn't noticed were surrounding him parroted back in a single voice.

Chapter 13

Yay

Hong Nori Lin was quite happy to have spent two hours alone in the tech booth side of the entry room of the SCIF with his boss' daughter. While Captain Samantha Sanders, Army CID, and stone cold judge of character had almost given in to his attempts for an after hours exploration of the local bars just three times, he felt tonight may be the night. He was guessing her weakness was karaoke and vodka with Red Bull shots.

Sitting in a small room off the exterior entryway of the SCIF with an attractive woman, Nori was in his element. They had been reviewing weeks and weeks of footage of the docks around the port on the center two monitors while slamming energy drinks and eating popcorn. Their work was a last check and balance to both verify whether they had the right ship, which they were confident of, but also to ensure they had the ONLY ship.

Nori paused with a handful of salted kernels as he saw something on a side monitor on the outside of the building. As they had been working out of the SCIF for the last month, he had a good feeling about the normal activities. His instincts kicked into play. Bobbling headlights did their usual to show a substantial inbound force. The vector of that force was on them.

At the far and attempted to be forgotten end of the Tori Station lands among a handful of other currently unused SCIFs, and given what his teams were there on base to do, there were only two potential outcomes. Someone was coming to shut them down or take them out.

Not liking either plan, Hong snapped a kiss onto Sam's cheek, avoided her slap back at the unexpected contact, sprinted the fifteen feet for the main panel, and then cut the power to their building.

As the emergency lights kicked in and Sander's string of salty curses trailed off, he heard her holster break and a press check to verify a round in the chamber. He knew the firearm wasn't pointed at him. She was neither stupid nor naïve. Which was why he kind of liked her.

"Talk to me, Hong!"

Playing back the images he'd tracked in his weak side eye peripheral, he was still confident. "Ten trucks, inbound on us."

"And that was why you cut the power?" Sanders asked.

"It's a SCIF," Hong pointed to the ocular and palm scanners on the reinforced bulkhead behind him. "And since we're about to do something hinky, and most of the people about to do that something are inside... SCIF rules apply. No? They can go out the back door while we delay whatever's going to happen."

Sanders took a deep breath, then took several steps to her

right and crouched behind a stout metal desk. Four stout bangs from a rifle butt sounded out against the outer door. Sanders looked over at Hong, who had taken up a similar position to hers, around eight feet to her left, except he didn't have a gun.

"What the heck did you DO, Hong Nori?"

*****

"What the heck did you DO?"

Olivia spat her question out, her glare directed at MD. Seeing his emphatic shrug in the dull red glow of her flashlight and accepting it as a universally communicated response. It wasn't me!

Olivia went back to the basics as most of the people in the darkened room clicked on personal lights to add to the dull emergency illumination. Most were ready for action, but were listening for direction. Her voice switched from the close quarters jab at MD to a shrill level blanket of sound.

"All teams fall back to rooms and lockers and prepare gear for immediate initiation. Pack for mission, as planned. All teams; back here in five!"

Olivia waited a moment to verify that the troops were indeed heading towards the hallways, then grabbed MD's shoulder.

"Something's wrong." Olivia hissed, before following her own orders and running towards her bunk and locker.

*****

"What's wrong?" Nori asked over the primary base Military Police channel.

"We need to make entry and secure this facility," a young MP LT called back. "Why is the power out?"

"I don't know," Hong lied. "We thought you all cut it. Or the storm coming or something. We can't open the door without power. Have you checked with the base command?"

"They sent us here!"

The poor guy fumbled with his phone for a moment before reading off the order. "Go to building C97, secure entry expedited, and detain all persons until relieved."

Hong let an anime styled laugh go out over the radio. "You just read out your orders over the radio? While, by my grandfather's soul, I must ask, how was that useful?"

"So, are you going to open the door?"

Hong held up a hand with four fingers to Sanders. "I am first, not allowed to open the door to you." He flashed a three. "Nor am I under orders to do so." A two fingered wave in the air. "And last, I can't open the inner door, since the power is off." One finger, and then an emphatic point at the deck.

Sanders, while still on the outs with the current process, respected Nori enough in their brief time to follow his lead. She dropped under the desk, tucked herself into a ball, and closed her eyes. Just a moment later, a complete light show fired off from the devices the RDI team had installed on the outer sheathing under the roof overhang of the building. In their minimal ability to see outside the outer office, those devices illuminated squads of armed soldiers, one of which had been moving towards the main door of the building with flash-bangs already cooking to affect entry.

The distractions of a few hundred million candlepower strobes threw off the game, and bangs punctuated the failed rush as the primed devices had to be ditched. Clouds of propellent from the explosive devices mixed with the lights to add to the optical diffraction and the acrid smell of burned powder to the air.

"The rest of the party is locked in," Nori called out into the dark. "We are not as blessed. I'd recommend staying low."

"Ya think?" Sam spat back as automatic fire began taking out the light show devices on the outside of the building.

*****

Before Olivia entered the main meeting room of the core facility with her bag, another female voice screamed out.

"I need a line, back way out people! Follow me, and pass on the path!"

"Was that PO Smith?" someone from Team X asked next to her in the hallway.

Before she could answer, the sounds of gunfire inside the facility shuffled dust down from the ceiling.

"Assume it's good," Olivia said. Then at the top of her lungs, she yelled the order, hoping it made it back out towards the rooms. "FOLLOW Petty Officer SMITH! ALL TEAMS: GO!"

That order on radio and via shouts smoothly galvanized the group. And as PO smith was aware of the critical tunnel system for this very building, she guided the entire contingent out to an opening on a cove close to Kadena Marina.

*****

The exterior door was forced in and MPs poured into the external security office. In moments, Sam and Nori raised their hands and were placed in flexi-cuffs.

The MPs did some door banging, flashed around with their lights a bit, found the power panel and then tried for a few moments to get the main breaker back up. The quick work Nori had managed with the plastic box rendered it useless without a replacement part. Several teams went into the exterior hallways around the core SCIF, and two went down the stairs to the facility room.

"Uh, dispatch?" one MP of the eight covering Sam and Nori called out over their radio. "We're in the entryway with two in custody, but the SCIF door is busted. We need an electrician and maybe an engineer to bypass."

Sam nodded to Nori in the dim corner, made sure he saw it, and then slammed out of her restraints and fired an axe elbow at the back of the neck of the MP in front of her.

We're doing this! Nori thought, performing a similar escape maneuver enabled by the too-tight cuffs and throwing himself at the two nearest.

The darkness helped, and no one dared to take a shot in the muddle of shadows, limbs, thrown objects from any surface at hand and splattering of blood. One MP got out her baton and smashed Sam on the side of the head, but she deflected most of the blow with her offhand and ducked around the repeat, snapped out a kick which likely broke the woman's knee.

Nori weaved through the darkness and was nearly untouchable. While his skill set drew heavily from a mix of martial arts, his focus in that leaning tended towards the killing blows. Not wanting to end anyone just following orders required him to hold back and go for less lethal disabling shots. He still left three MPs out cold, one with likely a concussion from a knee to the side of the head, two rolling around with kidney strikes, groin shots and several broken bones.

Breathing heavily, Sam took three duty belts off the fallen, passing two to Nori. He grabbed them, added his own gear, and followed her outside. At the last moment, Nori turned back around and snagged a pair of the MP's helmets nearest the door, flashed a light around at the carnage of the room, and smiled.

"I have an idea." Nori took off towards the farthest Humvee and had it spinning off before Sam could get her door closed.

"What are we doing?" Sam frowned. "They likely have the gates sealed."

"Not going to get out," Nori said.

He grinned over at Sam. Taking a hard left and towards the housing section of the base, Nori found the address he sought. A large officer's house with no car in the drive and one light on in the front living room. He parked the Humvee a few doors down behind a sports car under a tarp and went for his target door.

Picking the crappy base lock took him only a moment with his bump key and rubber band.

"Whose house is this?" Sam asked.

"Base commander," Nori said.

They both ducked as a strike of lightning hit nearby and the clouds opened up. Inside, Nori went straight for the kitchen, acquired a laptop which was plugged in on the counter, and opened it up.

"It's okay," Nori waved Sam to take a seat. "He lives alone. We snooped around a bit the first week he was here. Olivia and Trevor didn't really trust him."

Linking his laptop to the commander's, he fired up some software which began a clone. That started, he pulled a first aid kit from his pack, activated a pair of ice packs with pops and a shake, and passed them to Sam.

"Anything hurt other than the face?"

Shrugging, she placed one pack on her face and used the other one for her right hand knuckles.

"So what's the plan?"

"Assuming Olivia gets our gaggle past the south gate to the commercial docks, we may or may not have leverage to get out there. We knew there were tunnels under that building, but didn't expect to need them. Likely from WWII."

"Do I want to know?"

"It's best," Nori opened the fridge, took out a pair of beers and set them on the counter. "It's probably best if I don't tell you. You'd have to report it."

Raising an eyebrow, she shook her head at the beers.

"Figured," Nori put one back, extracted a can of Red Bull and mixed it with an expensive vodka in a glass. He located a charcuterie board under the bar and began setting out an artful array of crackers, meats and cheeses from the commander's well stocked fridge and pantry. "Once out the gate, they walk a few blocks to where we have a truck and trailer stashed. It may take two trips to shuffle everyone, but they will vanish into the night. We had already planned on a stealth exit in the morning."

"And why are we preparing a feast instead of going?" Sam readjusted the ice pack. "Not afraid of a little water, are you?"

They both jumped a little as a crack echoed against the windows of the house. The thunder followed immediately.

Nori pointed the knife at the sky.

"Zeus pissed," wiping off the blade, he moved on to a package of goat cheese from Finland. "Nah, I'm here to send a message. And I kind of need your help to do it. We should be able to easily get off base and join up in the morning after this storm clears."

The board was set up like something at a \$500/head wine tasting event by a master chef. Sliding it with a mini bow into the center of the small table, he turned and acquired the drinks, popping off the beer top on the counter's edge.

Sam glanced over at the laptops, filenames scrolling by in a small font. "I take it you need proof of him calling down his MPs to lock us in."

"And then I'll give him two choices." Nori sipped the beer and winced. "Sorry, he didn't have any wine. Not sure the French cheese will go with your caffeine infused heart attack."

Nori pointed out the stack of French cheeses, topped by a skillfully cut star in a piece of salami. Sam selected a different option. "And those options are?"

"He can decide whether to suck a nine millimeter, or you arrest him. That also sort of depends on the intel. If all he was trying to do was, say, put us on pause for him to figure out what we were up to; maybe he gets a pass. Interference, on the defense."

"Automatic first down. Move the chains," Sam nodded. "But if he wanted to put you in a hole?"

"I'll let you pick. Heck," Nori bowed. "Great first date material. Hey, my new boyfriend gave me the chance of letting a corrupt general off himself or allow me to get credit for busting his ass."

Sam pointed a piece of rather fragrant cheese at Nori in

warning. "Normally, buddy, the girl gets to pick the food. Boy pays. They get drunk and THEN get in a bar fight. You're doing this all backwards. Besides, I haven't said yes yet."

"That's because you won't get up the nerve to ask Olivia to borrow a dress."

"Oh, I have an outfit, and even a place picked out, Nori." Sam said. "I haven't decided whether you can handle me."

Nori's laptop dinged a cheerful sound, and he recovered it from the counter and began pouring through emails. They snacked and read while the storm raged.

Chapter 14

Roof

"This was the spot."

Molly knelt down to examine scuff marks on the hot tar. Taking her helmet off and gulping a sip of water, she took a few deep breaths, adjusted her plate carrier, and almost dropped her rifle while trying to shrug it off. With her mind completely consumed by analyzing the roof, she didn't have enough resources left to make the physical actions go smoothly.

"Okay there, ma'am?" Timmons asked. He stepped between her and the fireteam who moved around the roof behind them.

Molly said nothing for a moment as she focused her efforts on getting her pack off. A few clicks on the touchscreen on the box in the pack and she got back up to her feet slowly.

"I will be."

Her breath was even, and her phone was out and connected to the BattleBox. "Can you have that corporal with the fingerprint kit take a close look at that lawn chair?"

The chair looked good to her for a few reasons. First, it

had been dragged from its usual spot on the opposite side of the roof recently, as confirmed by the empty divots in the roof tar between two of such similar chairs. Second, it was pointed right at the Godmother's demolished brownstone, albeit blocked by trees and a few streets of houses.

Molly snapped a few pictures of scuff marks and began piecing together the details. Packages likely stacked to the left, where some square imprints on the soft surface and some transfer from a fabric based tape remained. Landing zone nearer to the center, with scrape marks, dents and scuffs of several landing and takeoff events. She waved for another soldier from the admin team to put a broken bit of drone prop in a bag.

"Corporal, can you take some scrapings around here too? Look for the tape fragments. And get an explosive analysis done?"

"Of course, ma'am."

"Hobb's intel was spot on," Timmons observed, and pulled a fresh breakfast burrito wrapper from the tar. Molly saw the movement out of the corner of her eye and watched the wrapper and the glove used to pick it up to go into a bag. "Also, this wrap came from a Circle-K."

"Then we have our next step in the game. Finding where the person got breakfast gives us a direction to track him."

Molly heard a beep from her phone. The notification indicated that the BattleBox had completed its survey of the local wireless networks and cell towers. "This may take a moment. Can you find the nearest of those gas stations?"

"Already have the list out." Timmons watched Molly draw her laptop out of her bag and limp over to one of the lawn chairs. "I'll call them and see which ones served bacon, egg, and cheese yesterday morning."

With the laptop open, water sipped, and scan results processed, Molly began the next step of harvesting the logs she could access. An issue with a lot of cell phones is they chat out and broadcast all kinds of useful information as they encounter radio networks. All it took was for a single one of those wireless networks to be protected by the default password and she could get a complete list of all radios which tried to connect. Cut out the normal serial numbers from the history, and she could narrow it down to the person or persons who were on the roof the day before at the time of the bombing.

After fifteen minutes, Molly had her list.

"Okay, from this, I can actually get the exact make and model of the drone used in the attack. Also, I have the cell phone number of the drone pilot. Or, likely, his cell phone number."

"Chance we can track it?" Timmons asked.

"Eh," Molly frowned. "Not sure I have the access, but I can tell if we're in range and likely triangulate it. And we have access to people who likely can make an intensive trace."

"That's still helpful. Also, we narrowed it down to two Circle-K's. One north of here, near Peabody, and the other south in Hingham."

"You take one, I take the other?"

Timmons shook his head. "You've got the cool little doom box of tricks, miss. Also, I'm pretty sure your big guy would try to take my head off if he found out I wasn't watching you. He looks mean. And I don't want to turn into a human Pez dispenser."

"Defensive end," Molly let a little smile out, accepted her pack from Timmons and slid in her laptop. "It's the one down in Hingham."

"How do you know, or are you guessing?"

Molly shouldered her rifle sling as she stood, wincing slightly as she thought ahead to the stairs down.

"Bit of both. The 508 area code is normally on the south side of the state. Also, the list I had access to has seen the same number and Wi-Fi radio before."

"When was that?"

Molly shook her head. "I don't know. I'd have to ask Jason for the source document. All I have is a summary. Some of the phone details were in a log of suspect IDs, sorted by zip codes and dates. Since the phone number is normally from the south, and seen in the south recently; we go south."

"To Hingham then."

Timmons held the door open for Molly and was about to offer to take her pack when she paused and held her side. One of his team had noticed the pause and stepped back a few to make a show of being busy.

"Sorry to say this," Timmons spoke softly after a few moments. "You three... Are not okay. Sure you should be out here?"

"Has Jason told you what happened?"

"Why is one of the best surfer dudes I served with in a wheelchair?" Timmons said. "Jason was always at the front of Charlie Company's runs. Always. Even when he was fighting off the flu, that kid would haul ass and inspire people to do better. Seeing him broken up like this hurts us all, but we will never ask. It's up someone who was there to deliver the story."

"Since I was there, can I tell you?" Molly resumed the stairs, leaning on the railing a bit more than she wished.

"That's different. Probably," Timmons cracked a smile. "Definitely, if it involves something embarrassing!"

"The three of us got hunted down by a battalion of forces," Molly summarized. "We got caught between two of their platoons and Jason was cut down. Took all night to break contact, but we knew Jason was going to die if we didn't get him help. Called for an extraction, but the helicopter couldn't take Brian and me because of fuel and weight."

"That sounds like an awful night."

"It was," Molly gathered speed at the next landing. "Unfortunately, they cornered us and we made a stand. Was just us 2 vs 45, plus some local law enforcement, though I think they just drove vehicles and tried to follow orders. Was in the news a bit, and there's a video on YouTube."

"Thank you," Timmons touched her shoulder.

"For what?"

"Getting our boy out," Timmons' voice hardened. "I kind of figured you three had been into something together, watching you move and communicate without words. You didn't answer my question, though. Should you be here?"

"Best place to be," Molly smiled over her shoulder. "Doing the right thing."

For whom? Timmons thought to himself.

Chapter 15

Door knocking

"Are you sure?" Hobbs asked the kid, a twenty folded up under his arm and ready to flash out with no one seeing.

"Yes, sir! Many drones. Amazon Freight Line in the sky!" a kid said.

Hobbs snuck the bill out and let it get snapped up by young fingers. The gaggle of kids fled after their ringleader in crime extorted their toll.

"Who's that tramping on my bridge?" Brian spoke softly behind Hobbs and caused the man to flinch.

"SHIT, I didn't even know you were behind me!"

Hobbs shook off the surprise, then did a double take as Brian Deegan was one of the Army contingent he had immediately realized wasn't finished with him over the legal scrape from months ago between him and Molly.

Brian had no malice in his genuine laughter.

"Sorry, Detective. Just... I can't even. They literally troll bridged your wallet there." The large man bent over slightly and held his stomach. "Ouch, that hurts."

"You okay?"

After a few breaths, Brian canceled the fit of laughter.

"For values of. Are we checking the other pack next door? Or are you out of bills? You realize they've all already coordinated and are going to try the same line. Some kids have been repeating the last two houses."

Hobbs looked at Brian and nodded slowly.

"And that was part of why I was so careful. Details matter to an investigation. Sometimes getting details out means acting like you are lost in the winds of life. Compare the consistent parts of ten different stories to the differences and you gain a view. Make it seem like you're being taken advantage of, and people oversell in the excitement."

Brian agreed and paced next to Hobbs as he walked towards the park on the corner of the street.

"The light steps which you didn't hear. It's simple. I took ballet as a kid. Once you get it into your muscles, it never really leaves, even while sporting size 15 boots."

Hobbs looked over at the large man, boggled for a moment, and shook it off.

"You must be joking. Ballet?"

"Dead serious. My aunt demanded it," Brian said. He then spotted something out of the corner of his eye on the street ahead of them. "DOWN!"

The detective spun about for a moment, looking for danger behind him, but had his wind knocked out of him as Brian smacked into him and then carried the man three steps down a basement apartment stair. Shots fired out in the middle of the movement and Brian grunted as one hit impacted his plates.

"Fire teams, contact!" Brian immediately called out on

comms to the ODA 3435 squads with them. "Shooter RIGHT, at my 2 o'clock, close. Old Ford explorer, silver. On ME! Going!"

After his command, Brian charged up the steps and sprinted across the street to the car with the shooter. The unexpected and fast approach on the shooter had caught the man in the hoodie and the sub-machine gun aiming at the team following Brian and Hobbs. With a yank and a smack of the shooter's head against the rear pillar, that shooter was out cold.

"Team C, contact, behind you," one other called, and Brian looked back to see a pair of guys in average clothes getting dragged out of a civilian Crown Victoria.

"Find the others!" Brian ordered, ducking low and scanning. Hobbs made the misfortune of poking his head out of the basement stair and Brian spotted a complementary motion ahead of them.

"Anyone have a shot? Four doors ahead of my position?" Brian asked.

As no instant answer came over the radio, Brian picked up a stone from the landscaping of the brownstone near them and sent it with all of his will towards the closest of the two men who got out of an SUV with rifles down the road. His aim was a bit off, but rather than striking the man in the face where he had aimed, it hit his throat.

An unexpected 4 pound paver striking your throat at over 80 MPH will simply crush. The man forgot about firing on Hobbs, who was in his sights, crashed to his knees, and attempted to figure out what was going on as he suddenly lost his ability to perform the critical act of taking air into his body.

The second figure saw the throw and fired a burst of automatic pistol caliber fire in Brian's general direction. The issue was, Brian and two of the opposing fire team members all had him in their range and answered back with several thumps of rifle rounds. The shooter crumpled.

"C, clear high. B, forward. H, pull up and protect the LEO," Brian ordered, moving forward but constantly checking his corners, looking at the windows and roofs around them. A pair of fire team C passed him, and he followed their cover to the man who was choking to death on the ground. Two more fire teams spread out to cover the road, centered on Brian.

Brian cursed twice under his breath, and then waved Hobbs up from the stairs.

"Crap. Call this guy a bus."

Hobbs rose but stayed low, walking forward while calling in the requisite "shots fired" announcement on his police radio and requesting EMS. He crawled the last few feet to Brian's location.

"Know CPR?" Brian huffed, well into his fourth set. "Don't bother with breathing. Just do 30 and check. Fast pace. Imagine the right song and go."

"Of course," Hobbs said.

"Can you take over?" Brian asked. He missed a beat while looking around, only to find that Charlie Company's squads had already moved up their vehicles, and one squeaked to a halt only feet from him to add to their cover.

Hobbs hesitated for a moment but then swapped in on the chest of the fallen man who was turning blue after the strike to the throat from the large stone launched at Mach 'eff you' velocity.

"Is this even going to work?" Hobbs asked. His words bounced in pitch with the effort of performing CPR.

"Do you want the chance to question him? Or not?" Brian looked carefully at the rooftops and then scrolled through the cars ahead of them. "All teams, what do you feel? Safe? Or should we bolt?"

The corporal from H replied. "While that ambush was weird, we have two secured in flex cuffs back in a hummer. We're worried about penetration, and will maintain space. I suggest we wait until EMS is here before moving up."

"I hate cars for cover," Brian frowned, set his rifle up on the hood of the Humvee closest and looked up at the left. "MRAP, can you prepare to fire on the top of the building on the left-hand side, three ahead of my current position? The brown one past the faded blue house."

"Adjusting," the driver said.

The large MRAP backed up a few feet and then turned into a driveway to get more angle. Brian heard the squeak of brakes and the gentle lope of the engine settling back to idle.

"Are you guys good?" Jason called over the radio. "We're one street over."

"A drone would be nice. Something to clear the roofs. Wait one," Brian slung his rifle, crossed quickly back over to the loose paver stones from the walkway, and acquired a second projectile.

"Gunner on the MRAP to lead," a voice called out. "I see a structure on that rooftop. It looks like a little plastic garden shed. There are some metal planters next to the roof edge."

"Yup." Brian could make out the peak of the shed. "I'm going to try to hit it."

"With what?"

Brian drew back and lobbed the stone. It arched up high in the air over the street and smashed against the third floor wall just below the roofline. As Brian knelt to steal a third projectile, a cackle of gunfire reached down, popping holes in the car in front of him. Brian dove for the engine block.

Already aimed in, the .50 BMG M2 Browning on the MRAP opened up. That answering heavy automatic fire tore the rooftop hide to pieces.

"Check fire," Brian called. "Captain, can you send forces in to check the structure? It's brown, um. Address number is one-eight. It's seven back from the next crossroad. We just shot up some guys on the roof."

"On it," Jason replied. "Knocking on the door in twenty seconds. All teams on your side hold till we clear to prevent crossing the streams."

A fire truck had pulled up behind them. At the sounds of gunfire, it backed back down the road to a cross street. A police SUV paused near the front of the MRAP with the window rolled down. The officer was staring blankly at the still smoking barrel of the turret.

Crossing to Hobbs, who had switched out with a sergeant keeping up CPR, Brian thought for a moment, looked over at the back of the Humvee, and motioned for one of the other ODA to bring up the one behind them.

"Let's get this guy in and back out of the road."

It took a bit of bashing on the hatch lid to open the back, but they moved the injured into the rear in a brief shuffle.

The same private went back to chest compressions while they backed the vehicle all the way out of the road to the fire truck and now waiting ambulance.

"All clear," a sergeant said. "Two dead on the roof. Looks like they've been up here a while on watch. They had keys to the third-floor apartment and we're sweeping that unit now. Confirm six bunks, six bedrolls, six toothbrushes."

"And since we have six dudes, we are likely clear," Brian said.

Brian added up the body count.

"Hobbs, you good to coordinate with passing this scene off to locals, or do I have to do it?" Jason asked.

Brian looked over at Hobbs, who checked his belt and noted the second radio for their system was missing. Brian unclipped his mic and held it out to the man.

Hobbs shook a little and sat back against the truck. "I'll handle it. Just give me a moment."

"First time in a firefight?" Brian asked.

"First time in an ambush!"

Hobbs shook it off, stood and pulled out his notepad while he walked over to the patrol car.

"Damn it, that shit was scary."

A few moments for him to collect his notes in the passenger seat with the air conditioning on full blast and he launched into the coordination.

Chapter 16

The Concerned

"Damn it!" Olivia complained, tossing her day pack in the box truck and wringing out her floppy hat. The button down, loose fitting over-shirt similarly twisted to remove water. She laid it over her pack and turned to glare at MD. "I had just washed my hair, too."

"I can't control the weather," he frowned, scooting in more.

Michael plopped down on the dusty floor of the old truck and crushed in next to MD in the cramped space. From the front, Collin and one of the New Mexico RDI team had gotten their safety lockout to prevent theft removed and had the engine started.

"Nor, it seems, can I handle one potentially corrupt base commander. I was hoping Sam would be enough to get a full special secret government Project Litmus Test background test on him. Seems there's so much of a backup it'll take half a year."

"That's sort of your fault, MD" Olivia checked her chest and crossed her arms.

PO Smith had come to the briefing in her uniform blouse

and pants because of the hundred degree plus weather. As such, when the rain began pouring on their mile walk through a rather crowded corner of the island near the marina, she had a problem. Her headlights had been on. It was bad.

Olivia had taken pity on the woman and loaned her the hardshell off her own back. Giving her glare to MD one more notch on her, "I am a displeased woman; it's your fault" scale and checking to make sure his eyes weren't looking at her own wet chest, she tapped the wall of the box with her knee.

Randy Wakeman closed the door of the truck and gave a thumbs up in her direction.

"Ready, Collin," Olivia said.

Her glare softened, and she moved on to other business as they started moving.

"Any word from Nori and Sam?"

MD laughed, clicked open his phone from its waterproof pouch and showed her a picture.

"That kid is persistent. All in place. He's got General Berger's cell number and likely has an hour before the storm passes to make his findings and get a decision made between the three of them."

"Is that... a charcuterie board?" Michael asked about the spread in the picture.

"Boy is determined," Olivia said. She smirking at the timed picture Nori took with his hand gently touching Sam's, cheese and meats in full display in frame. "Wonder if he knows her preferences."

Damion groaned and rolled his eyes, coughed and got his back patted by a Seal riding with them.

"Didn't you date Sanders once?" Michael asked Damion.

The question caused Damion to cough again and wave his hand.

"I wouldn't call what happened dating." MD said. He looked over at the tall guy, struggling with his breath. "They hooked up at a Christmas party, or was it a BBQ? About a year ago. You okay there, Damion? Cat got your tongue?"

The man couldn't muster enough will to decide whether he was going to growl or cough again. Instead, he just set his head down in his hands and rolled it back and forth a bit.

"He found out he's allergic to cats," MD blinked in explanation. "And one of her cats attacked him when he sneezed into its face."

"Oh, that's funny," Olivia said. She let a smile warm her face as she leaned back against the metal, still warm from sitting in the sun all day despite the current rain. "If I didn't want to get my phone wet, I'd tap that out to his girlfriend, Cynthia, right now."

"I think we should give our poor guy here a bit of a break." Randy said.

"Yesh!"

In half an hour, they pulled into a muddy dock facility several miles off the beaten path. The poorly lit wharf jutted out well into a large bay to the north, with large fuel tanks behind them in the tropical forest. Next to a small dock sat a pair of 40 foot vans with their RHIBs inside, fuel and spare parts. Alongside those was a smaller 20 foot container with the bulk of their gear.

While the rain had stopped, the wind was dropping to nothing. The post-storm absence of breeze usually warned that the insects were about to come back out and hunt for night-time meals.

The Sandy Stewart was tied up next to the 40 foot vans, and her crane was out, already rigging up to the first container. Collin drove right up to the area near the vans, and everyone got out of the truck and trailer, one Seal team complaining about the rough ride in the stiffly sprung trailer unit made for hauling wood, not people.

"Thanks, Collin," Olivia checked her watch and waved for Damion to ride with him. "See you back with the second load in an hour?"

"I'll stop for gas," Collin nodded. "About an hour plus ten ish."

"Let us board, people!" Olivia said.

She spotted Trevor on the deck next to Cynthia watching the crane operation raise a hand in welcome. Olivia returned the warm wave, gathered her gear, and followed the line of wet teams.

Chapter 17

Day of Rest

While Davis and his 3430s were finishing up the salvage operation of the Brownstone, Jason found himself in a weird in-between place. The sudden shift from organization, planning and actions were replaced with the most dangerous of things; downtime. Since neither Molly nor Brian had been shooting since their mutual situation, and all three were now carrying rifles that meant business, the tickle of boredom pointed to Jason as a way of getting out of the weird. Putting steel down range was in order. Sun, sand, gunpowder and a summer breeze were on the menu. There was no replacement for thumps of explosions against one's chest in the open air.

Thanks to a quick call to local law enforcement, they had a private training range just outside of the I-495 circle all to themselves. ODA 3435 was running transition drills on the 50 meter range, but Jason had brought his party to the long range section.

BANG ... Ding! Brian grinned.

BANG ... <<silence>> Molly frowned and looked up from her optic.

BANG ... DING! Jason also smiled and lowered his M4 to the table, clearing it before turning to his friends.

"No hit?" Brian looked over at Molly.

Her face was a mix of frustration, anxiety, and a bit of pain. She made a quick adjustment to the M68 Aimpoint optic on the M4, reacquired the 100 yard gong target and fired off a round, which rang it. Briefly glaring down at the weapon, she made two more shots on the gong, both hits. Then she switched to the 200 yard plate and sent the rest of her magazine onto the target before setting the weapon down and then glaring at them.

Brian was a bit confused for a moment at the glare, but quickly realized when Jason was laughing his ass off that some mischief had been afoot.

"Did you?" Brian asked, but punted the rest of his question as Molly pulled out a multi-tool from her pack and began screwing off the muzzle device from her loaned M4.

Jason, still fighting a fit of snickers, nodded.

"Yes. Sorry, Molly. I... I couldn't help it."

Molly said nothing, and the two men watched as she finished resetting the combined brake and compensator from the upside down configuration back to where it was supposed to be, moved the gas block knob back to the non-suppressed mode, and then bore checked her optic. Last, she took the rubber wedge out of the back of the buffer tube, which was causing the recoil to be... off.

BANG ... DING.

Message sent, Molly put her weapon on safe and walked off the line to take a drink of water.

Jason and Brian exchanged a quick glance before taking

back up their arms to alternate shots on the much more manageable 100 yard target on the range. While they were shooting, Timmons sat on the bench next to Molly and nodded at her M4.

"They punked you?"

Molly shrugged and waved her left hand at her rifle on the table. "I sort of deserved it. Didn't notice Jason had messed with the brake and buffer when I went to the bathroom. That's on me for not expecting the prank."

"You're normally a rightie, correct?"

Holding up her cast, Molly examined her hand. "I'm thinking, not anymore. Right hand, and right eye dominant. My hand got really messed up."

"Are you happy with your setup?" Timmons continued his challenge. "Is it ready for what you need?"

Molly looked over at the older sergeant. Something about the tone made Molly both uncomfortable and bothered. Then she nodded.

"It's good enough," Molly sniffed. "I really prefer an 18 inch barrel, and a 1-6x or 1-8x optic to a red dot, but now that I've figured out what the boys did to it today, I'm good. I am glad to have gotten the chance to shoot it. Bit different from my personal 18-inch at home, or the rifle I carried in Baku."

Timmons stood, pulled a crisp $50 out of his pocket and set it on the shooting table in front of them, placing a 5.56 round on the bill to keep it from blowing away in the errant wind. "Challenge rules are off hand only. Best out of 5 at 600 yards."

Molly raised an eyebrow, and Jason and Brian both looked

back.

"I'm out," Brian waved off, slung his rifle and gathered his gear. "I'm going to head next door and take some time on the plate racks. Long distance is not my thing. Defiantly not offhand."

"What was your YouTube channel, Jason?" Molly asked.

"Chicsdig65!" Jason looked over at Molly, grinned a little and then began loading up a mag. "Best out of five, you say, Timmons?"

"Best out of five," Timmons agreed.

Molly stood up, walked to her rifle, inserted a fresh mag and chambered a round. Observing the long distance target in the open optic was easy, but with no marks in the view, the holdover would be all on her at this distance. She set her rifle down, still on safe. "You first."

Timmons stepped up, shouldered, flipped the selector to fire, and sent a round onto the 600 yard gong.

Molly carefully raised, paused, fired and hit. Noting it was high and left, she looked carefully for a few moments at the leaves and blades of grass to plant a picture of what the wind was doing in her mind.

Jason took a deep breath, focused, fired. And missed.

"Oh, it's on now, Richardson."

Timmons prepared his shot, took it, and missed.

Without a pause, Molly took her second and scored a hit, setting her rifle down and rolling out her right shoulder.

"She's in the lead," Timmons said. "Gonna let a girl beat you, Jason?"

Steel dinged, and Jason relaxed back down to his lap.

"You know, this isn't easy, Timmons. Why off hand?"

"You know why."

Timmons breathed and squeezed and scored a hit.

"Gonna have to step it up, Captain."

"Molly, I think Timmons may need some Crayons. Chance, you have any to spare?"

"I'm not a Marine," Timmons complained, looking over at the woman, observing how she moved. Molly took her shot and scored.

"Crap," Jason said. He frowned, shook himself, raised and relaxed. He smiled when his round barely kissed the lower edge of the steel. Still, a hit was a hit.

Timmons took his time with the next shot, letting his body melt into the hold with his hand wrapped around the rifle sling to help stabilize. The careful sequence managed a hit.

Molly snapped off a round only seconds after, and also scored, causing Jason to laugh. The timing of her shot so close to his obviously rattled Timmons.

Jason shook his head, shook out each hand, settled himself in and snapped off a ding.

"Crap," Timmons said. The echo of Jason's word was barely above a whisper. The sergeant was doing his best to reach for composure. Three breaths, one reset of stance, and then a shot. And a miss.

With a bow to Molly, Timmons watched her carefully as she took her time with her last shot. Waiting for the wind to drop back under the slight gusts which wiggled the grass, she squeezed and scored.

"Crap," Jason said, a bit more loudly. While he knew Molly had just beat him, he was even with Timmons. This would not do! His left leg was trying to do a cramping thing, his back was on fire, and he needed to take a piss.

Pushing all of those sensations aside, Jason looked over at Molly. Even though she had already won this little friendly competition, her expression was of focused concern. Concern for him. Could he make the shot? Jason looked over at Timmons, who was presenting a satisfied expression.

Jason decided simply; "I'm going to make this shot."

Three breaths, then four. The wind felt right, and the world felt right. Jason squeezed and hit steel.

Timmons, laughing, pulled the bill off the table and passed it to Molly.

"I will never forget getting my ass kicked by the Valkyrie of Baku. Five out of five at 600 long with a 14.5 inch barrel and a red dot? Damn."

"Nothing like working on the edge of your hardware," Jason said.

"If we take two more shots?" Timmons asked. He looked over his shoulder at the woman. "Would you go easy on me? Now that I'm dialed in?"

"Since you got three to my five," Molly said, then snickered. "Nope. Not happening. I won, boys."

Grinning, Jason set the barb. "I still beat your ass, Timmons."

"You asked the other day," Molly said. Her voice took on a low tone, barely audible in their ear protection. "Timmons. You asked why we were here? Why I was here? While I appreciate the head check, are you good with the results of your challenge?"

The man grunted, looked between the faces of the two,

and sighed. "You guys may be in recovery from getting the shit kicked out of you, but as I said. Damn. No worries."

"You know," Jason said, then smirked at Molly. "I'm going to have to challenge you now, to a proper bolt gun at a thousand, Molly."

The woman laughed at Jason's smirk, but shook her head. "Not my thing. You and Damion and Michael own that space."

Timmons locked eyes with Jason, and then slowly nodded his head. "Don't let this jumped up provisional title 32 rank shit get to your head, Jason. You're still barely more than a solid sergeant at the end of the march. Got me?"

"Wait, what?" Molly and Jason both asked at the same time.

"Couple of things," Timmons spoke softly, mirroring Molly's low tone. "I understand why Charlie Company was assigned over to you all, and I respect you. It's not usual for this sort of mission set to happen on US soil. Hence why I backed the range day to get to know each other."

"And then you got your hat handed to you by a pair of invalids."

"Oh, shove it up your ass," Timmons laughed at his own expense. "I'm trying to be serious here! Just reminding you two that we are outside the scope of norms."

"Maybe it's us who should do the lecturing then. Welcome to our world," Molly growled.

Timmons blinked at that response and then snorted in agreement. "Fair shot. Just keep in mind what I pointed out. Our worlds have collided. Let's keep them both intact until the end of the mission."

Jason held up a hand as his phone dinged and he checked the notification. "The demo team just found a bunch of cell phones and the BattleBox from the second floor office. They're sending the debris from that search grid to the warehouse now. Will be a few hours before they get the grid logged and ready to process. Let's grab lunch soon and head that way?"

"I've got seventeen rounds left in my mag," Molly looked over at Jason.

Jason pocketed his phone, checked his mag, and snorted. "Which target?"

"Why ask? All of them! Two hits on each."

"Ya'll have at it," Timmons slung his rifle with a smile. "I need to catch up on some email."

Molly and Jason spent the next few minutes slowly exchanging paired shots at all the gongs on the range. As expected; Molly won, even on her weak hand. Jason hung close to her, finally getting a high-five as he managed his last shot on the 600 before they packed up.

Timmons watched the two friends closely from the back bench in silence. The sun on his face meshed with the dispersed smell of spent gunpowder in a good way.

Chapter 18

Lightning

The god of the skies, Zeus, was mad. As a squall seemed to chase their ship around like a demented swarm of bees, the only thing that made Captain Santiago feel better about their situation was the fact that the typhoon's leading edge was going to pass a day's steam south of them. This venture had turned from a viable financial experience to a cruise from hell.

Another lightning strike just off their port bow made him wince, and he spilled his coffee cup.

The last two months had been tough on his seventeen crew. Random gremlins had struck the *Crystal Dream* hard. At just over 320 feet long and 65 across, she was a small ship for the open ocean. Modern systems were, by design, supposed to make up for her small size. Powerful engines, massive electrical systems, computer controlled emissions all gave her, on paper, an edge on larger vessels built in the old ways.

The lower estimated fuel costs alone offset the added vessel build expenses. Until stuff broke. And stuff was breaking at an alarming rate on his little ship. Santiago reviewed two more of those expense reports on the counter in front of him, shuffled the printouts of the parts delivery schedule for their next two long port calls in Manzanillo, Mexico for the following month and then Sri Lanka a month after that aside and focused his attention on the most pressing issue; the weather forecast. He honestly wasn't sure he could make it to Mexico to pickup spares before his dire situation became critical.

"I think we're going to have to head to Guam," Santiago said.

The second mate turned from the wheel and winced. "They will not like that. We'll miss a delivery."

"I know," Santiago penciled out a quick fuel calculation next to the storm track. He didn't bother going for a ruler. They had more than enough fuel to get to either Guam or Okinawa; not enough fuel to make it safely to Manzanillo because of issues with the engine's running poorly.

"Our employers were very adamant about us not returning to either of the closer ports after... something phase in their work. With all the issues we've had this month, I'm not sure I want to make for Mexico. Midway is an option, but expensive as hell."

"It's on their no-go list of major ports, too. Maybe Manila? I'll even offer to buy the first round of beers, captain."

Santiago nodded twice and moved to a computer screen to plug in a course simulation and check transit times.

"You just want to go there since you have a girl in port in Manila! I think that's the ticket, Jomari. But of course we can't do anything until this huge ass storm coming at us passes by. I'm guessing four, maybe five, days before we can turn around. Then we sneak past before the next typhoon."

"It's doing it again!" The panicked third engineer from the engine room called out on the ship intercom.

Santiago didn't fault her for forgetting radio discipline. They were a civilian crew, mostly skilled merchant marine sailors. The decades of experience and professionalism accounted for a lot, but when you had to stay up almost constantly because of a...

"Now it's like every five minutes, bridge," 3e repeated. "I could use a hand!"

"You just need someone to smack a reset button and flip a switch, right?"

"Yes, captain," 3e said. "Issue is, I need to clock out like now, and before I do that, I need to get down to pass some equipment to the chief engineer. I'd normally switch out with one of our wipers, since she can do this and cover the entire board, but she's literally covered in shit and clamping a bypass together in the hold so the chief can weld it up."

"Hang on," Captain nodded to an able-bodied seaman, Doug, who had just come up to the bridge to check on the shift change. "Doug, come here."

"Okay, explain it, 3e. The second mate can hear, and he's going to be in charge of the next helper. I'm about to send an AB down to you. So what's happening?"

"It's like a nuisance. Short is, once every five or ten minutes, a warning system fires off on our 24VDC main panel. The main motors are powered via are a direct drive from the engines. Issue is, that warning system will cut all power to our steering system and screws if it isn't acknowledged in time and reset. I'll show you. Uh... Damn it!"

The mic dropped as an alarm sounded in the background. A few moments later, 3e was back on.

"All well?"

"No," the woman's frown was communicated through the radio. Not one, but two sighs followed before she resumed speaking. "Just send him down. I'll show him the light and process. It's easy. Anyone can do it."

"And that other alarm?"

"Sorry, captain, the power generator for the 220 VAC used in the labs just went down again. I'll get it back up, but it takes a while to restart. Can't do that AND watch the panel, anyway. I need a hand."

"Great," the Captain signed off and turned to Doug. "Help her out?"

Doug nodded agreement, "I was supposed to be painting anyway this shift, can't exactly do that right at the moment since it's blowing thirty knots, can I? Sounds like all she needs is someone to just do like that little bird on the Simpsons? Push a button, flip a switch, watch a warning light?"

"Hit the spacebar; Doug. Thanks, son."

As the large man walked down the ladder, a very red faced gray-bearded South African scientist stomped up. Captain Santiago sighed as he knew what this was about.

"The fucking power is out; again! We just lost half a day's worth of work!"

Before he could even try to respond to the irate scientist who was running the onboard fabrication labs, half the lights on the bridge board indicating problems flashed on. He felt the shudder of the engines stop and the input from the bow thruster keeping them into the sea cut out.

The second mate reached for the radio with a groan after an exchanged a look with the captain.

"Um, engine room? We just lost our mains!"

Chapter 19

Choice

"That sounds like a slam dunk for a court martial," General Berger frowned into the camera, having read through the selected incriminating emails multiple times with Sam and Nori. Sitting in the early morning sun on his back deck in Virginia, he was occasionally having to field a rather chipper Malinois who was insistent on getting some ball time in as the dew burned off the grass.

Sam wished she didn't now have an image of one of the highest ranked officers in the armed services sipping coffee, wiping dog slobber off his hands, and wearing his PJs, but nothing could be helped.

"I wouldn't hesitate to put this in the hands of the JAGs, sir. Does this mean we have a go?"

"Captain Sanders, we have no choice but to act on this information, just as you suggested. It's a very unfortunate turn of events. Having reviewed the facts, I am cutting the orders for you to apprehend Brig. Gen. Paul R. Birch." Berger grunted as he threw a tennis ball on the end of a blue stick. "I'm sending David Nahom, Lieutenant General, to take the slot. He won't be there for..."

"Sir?"

"Sorry, captain, literally watching the little dots on my phone and waiting for the text message from the aircraft carrier to make its way. It's not in my job description to calculate flight times for an F15. Okay, eta in hand. Just over an hour. You'll like David. He's a solid guy."

"The data was all captured using RDI equipment, General Berger. I'll make sure we package up everything we find following existing protocols within their contracts. Of course, with my signature on the witness fields for each discovery."

"No concerns, Sanders," Berger said. "My office was already briefed that an investigation was underway. I'm sorry that events on base pushed the timeline ahead of the other mission. Life sometimes has other ideas in situations like this."

"Not to mention mother nature," Sam said. She ducked as the flash of light followed by a distant rumble of thunder. "We got hit pretty hard. I'm still jumpy."

"At least the winds keep away the bugs, captain. Both human and insect most times. Strange how that similarity shows through across species."

"Until the replacement, General Nahom, gets here, general, what should we do with the brigadier? I'm saying this as a lowly CID captain who got in a rather spicy scuffle with eight of his MPs just a few hours ago. We do not know how much of the base is out looking for us and our strike team."

"Are any of the military police dead?"

Sam looked over at Nori, who was off screen. He shrugged, and she made a face at him. "We don't think so."

"Then, consider it a bar fight. They were acting under orders. You were acting under orders. We sort it out in post production of the drama. Got me, Sanders?"

"Yes, sir," Sam raised a hand. "But what do we do with Birch in the meantime? He is likely to come home any minute."

Nori walked over and dropped one of the two MP helmets on her head.

"Sorted." Nori said, waved at the camera and then returned to his place in the corner next to the front door.

After a long sigh, and the removal of the stolen token of power from her head, Sam nodded. "We'll figure something out. How will General Nahom contact us?"

"I gave him your cell phone number," Berger said. His laugh was punctuated with another throw off camera. "Is that the same cool cat who was with Elizabeth O'Neal a few months ago who brought her and her kids down?"

Sam glowered briefly at the man across the living room, paused only for a moment to stare longer than she had intended at his well-toned butt, and then spoke with honesty. "Hong Nori Lin? He's a cat. That's for sure. I think it was him."

"Please have him call me when this is over. I have some information for him about his wife."

Sam raised her eyebrows, glanced up to see Nori wave his hand in a "later" gesture, and then nodded.

"Thank you, General Berger."

"A pleasure, as always, working with your family, Sam. Take care of yourself!" The general threw the gooey ball from one hand and cut the call with his other.

Sam stared at the screen for a few moments, looked over

at Hong Nori Lin, and spit out a single word, harsher than she had intended. "*Wife?!?*"

His gesture of "later" was repeated twice this time, and he ducked down next to the door and then backed into the closet. Lights from a car, which she hadn't noticed while distracted by the call, turned off outside. Cursing to herself, Sam slapped the laptop lid down and moved to the left to cover out of sight of the door with a taser in her hand from the stolen MP belt.

Lock shuffled, door opened, a man in uniform stepped in and flipped on the hall lights. He turned to hang his already removed belt on a hook. Nori spun out of the closet, divested the man of the duty belt, wrapped the body with his legs, and had Birch's neck wrenched so far over in the hold when Sam got to them she was afraid she was going to hear a snap.

She deployed flex cuffs and searched for concealed weapons. Tape acquired from the basement toolbox went into action and wrapped around limbs over the plastic ties to prevent the easy ways of removal that they had demonstrated earlier.

"I regret to inform you, General Birch, that you are being placed under arrest. We will hold you until your relief arrives with orders to take your command. Understand me, sir?"

At a brief nod from the bound man, Nori relaxed his crank.

"Wise choice, Birch." Nori gave the bundled man a tap on the shoulders. "Wise choice."

Chapter 20

Thunder

It had been a brutally long day at the warehouse, and Jason was exhausted. A private from the company had helped him bring a box of electronics back to their hotel. He had figured a shower, a room service burger and a lengthy hacking session would make him feel like he'd done something useful for the day.

Jason reinserted Cell Phone 7 into its labeled evidence bag and plugged in Cell Phone 8. This one was in better shape than some others, as it had fallen under the large desk and been shielded well by the dense old hardwood. As it was an older Chinese knock off of an Indian knockoff of a Motorola, it had been lowered on their punch list. That list had included reviewing the weeks of footage on the older BattleBox which had been in Godmother's comms closet, the security system hard drive, and her several generations of iPhones locked in a fireproof safe. The laptop had taken a bit of melted metal and the SSD was toast.

"The woman had a lot of phones," Jason said, kicking up the Android SDK and preparing to dump the phone onto the virtual machine on his laptop.

With a bite of his now cold burger in the hatch, he frowned down at the clone tool and then flipped his screen to a document they had uncovered that morning. It was a note on the first cell phone, the one Godmother had on a family plan with her daughters, and Jason had recalled that the 4 digits at the top of the quick note matched the IMEI on the 8th phone.

Rather than queuing up the program which had a low chance of cracking the pin on the android encryption in the next day or so, Jason tapped the nine-digit number from the line of the document onto the device. It booted right up and he was in.

Going straight for the text messages while the device cloned, Jason scrolled to the top of the list. One message hadn't been sent. It read:

> *James Weatherly just called me. It's him. How did we miss this?*

What next surprised Jason was that there was an SD card full of recorded audio in the phone. Checking the storage port, he noticed that someone had covered the microSD card with some sort of hard adhesive. Since the transfer rate off of the device was horrifically slow, getting the 128GB card out and directly accessing it would be the only way he could get more data fast. He would not wait all night for what should take only a few minutes.

A scrape of his knife blade cleared the glue and the small card popped out. However, he didn't have an adapter handy.

Wheeling to the door, he crossed the hall and paused. It was just past 2300 hours. Taking a deep breath and hoping some of the fun they had at the range would prevent Molly from being pissed if he woke her up, he knocked on her door. The sounds of a news broadcast could be heard through the thin wood.

After a brief shuffle inside, the door opened, and Brian poked his head out. No shirt, flannel pajama pants and a Glock in his hand, tactfully lowered, completed his outfit.

"Um," Jason, confused. "I expected someone smaller and better looking. Also, less naked."

"What's up?"

"I," Jason cocked his head as a light went on and he saw movement back in the room. "Any chance I can borrow a card reader? I have an SD card reader with me, but I left my multi port adapter back at the warehouse and I need a micro."

In seconds, Molly, wrapped in a thin robe with her hair wet, walked to the door and passed Jason a small device with a cord hanging off the back.

"Good?" Brian asked.

Checking the ports on the device, Jason nodded, dropped it into his lap, and looked up at the two.

"Good."

Jason stated as blankly as he could manage, turned, and waved a goodnight over his shoulder.

He made it most of the way towards his door and heard the click of the latch behind him before he let the laugh he had been trying to squelch burst free.

"I HEARD THAT!" Molly called out from her room.

Jason's snickering continued as he badged back in and began the download of audio recordings.

The folder where the recordings were stored was an artifact of a software package which automated recordings of phone calls. The earliest one dated back over seven years. While the copy continued, Jason went to the minibar, pulled out a beer, and popped the top.

Almost an hour later, Jason had reviewed several phone calls, including a rather spicy exchange between MD and the Godmother, and found what he believed was her last call. That call, plus the interrupted text message, was enough for him to need guidance from his team leader. He had to make a phone call himself.

A brief twinge of panic suddenly gripped his chest as he raised his cellphone off the desk. After all, the last person who attempted to pass on this message over a cellphone ended up dead.

Setting the device down and shaking his head, he put on his headset and instead called through a comms app over the VPN tunnel through the hotel network.

On the third ring, one of the RDI service interchanges cycled in and then the encrypted call was shuffled to best-means. A satellite dropped the call feed onto the ship that Olivia was riding out of Okinawa, and then local Wi-Fi to her device. Olivia picked up.

"Go ahead," her voice sounded slightly labored, and Jason heard a splash of water and then rustling of cloth. "Jason?"

"Ya, it is I," Jason said. He played back the sequence of events briefly, formulated a summary of questions about the audio files, and opened his mouth. Then somehow that mouth made other sounds than planned. "Did you know that Molly and Brian are sleeping together?"

"Collin told me," Olivia said. Her reply was sharp, and the signal broke for a second as she switched the call to her laptop and opened her video. He reflexively followed suit just in time for her to see Jason's reaction to the fact that she knew about the relationship change and catch the tail end of his own emotional response to acknowledging it.

"Did he?"

"I mean, you knew they had been living together for the last few months, right kid?" Olivia admonished. "What did you expect to happen? Girl, boy; house... Bed?"

Jason knew she was trying to tease him a little, but he found his ground.

"I knew it could happen. Knew it might happen, and actually, am glad for it. Not the reason I called. Just... caught me by surprise."

"But it was the first thing you spoke about?" Olivia raised an eyebrow, wiped sweat from her forehead and demanded clarification with one of her patented glowers.

"I think a part of me needed to make sure that you knew," Jason said. He gave an honest shrug and waved it off. "I called for a potentially serious topic. You know what we're doing up here in Mass, right?"

"MD and Trevor have read me in." Olivia let the other part go for a bit.

"I'm completely convinced that Josiah colluded to put me here to make sure there is an officially verifiable sharpie mark drawn towards a person who he pointed me at a few days ago."

"Go on."

"Does the phrase 'You're not hearing me' mean anything

to you? Specifically? As it was issued from the person who last spoke to the Godmother."

Olivia considered it briefly.

"Hang on, I should get MD, particularly before you say the name."

The low resolution video swung around the room, which looked like a dingy lab crossed with a wheel and tire shop you wanted to avoid. In the new visual, a round portal could be seen. A wave crashed over the glass, causing some water to dribble down and a spray flashed across the camera.

"Drat," Olivia wiped it off and then moved her laptop further from the spray zone. MD, hair wet and grease on his face, wearing a hard hat and work vest entered from the back, unsteady on his feet, and managed to sort of not fall on Olivia as she took a spot on a stool. "Sorry, kid, we're on a snotty path, trying to get around a typhoon. We had to take a slight detour to pick up Sam and Nori on our way out and missed the tide. Seas are worse now, smoother later once we get around the weather."

"What's up?" MD dropped his hard hat into a rack on the back wall.

"MD, is Olivia cleared for my op?"

"Go, kid."

"James Weatherly. I'm fairly convinced he was the one who killed the godmother. Also, because of Josiah's hint; likely the same person who assassinated the Ulysses CEO."

"Never met him," MD said. "And actually never even heard of him in any circle as directly involved in pretty much anything, even though he was the CSO of Ulysses. Kind of odd for someone in that position to never mingle with the others in the field."

"Like Josiah hinted, this guy was a shell. Anyhow, Molly could piece together with the help of some of the army engineering dudes how the hit happened. This guy dropped a few hundred small boxes on her roof with a drone. Probably took him like half the morning slowly delivering them one at a time. Then when he wanted to, called her up for a classic evil villain's final 'I'm going to blab at you and then kill you' speech. And then initiated the boxes of explosives."

"Ouch," MD sniffed.

"Did you know the Godmother had been recording a ton of calls?"

"Most of her stuff was recorded and compartmentalized to grants or projects. So, ya. I always do the same at that level. Prevents confusion. Some people never hear what's spoken the same as others."

"I was not talking about the official record keeping software. She captured audio on a cell phone," Jason held up the slightly cracked Phone 8. "Compressed audio. Not even complete sequences. It's also the sim card Weatherly texted her on."

"What was the number?" Olivia opened up a document on her phone.

Jason called out the digits. MD cursed, and Olivia highlighted the same number in the document and showed MD to confirm.

"This is bad, this is very bad," MD said. He shook his head, and leaned back as a wave moved the ship, causing him to stabilize on a bench with a hip.

"Maybe." Olivia tapped her mouth with her fingers. "Maybe

not. Do you all know the scene in 13 hours of Benghazi where the 17th Feb commander, they are the good guys in the history, calls up the enemy commander on his cell phone? He says something to the effect that he knows all the bad guy's numbers."

"It's been a while since I've watched the movie, but I remember it," MD said. "Your point?"

"Ah," Jason laughed. "Heck, that movie got me laid last week. I think her point, MD is, maybe Godmother, like the 17Feb commander was on our side, and like him, was on some sort of call list with other people who play at the same level. Sort of like baseball teams. You may hate the ball team next door, but you might have the coach's number so you can call them up and arrange a pickup game."

"While this list of unknown numbers is a suspected naughty list of sorts, these numbers aren't vetted or identified. Just potentially suspect in a bad way."

"Wasn't this the same commander in the movie, the idiot who left the back gate open?" MD contemplated the ramifications.

"Yup." Jason took a deep breath. "Did the godmother leave the back gate open? Or was she involved?"

"I think we should round table this, Frances. Get a level set of what Godmother knew we were doing on a board, and then make some tweaks. Change things up a bit."

"Agreed, Olivia," MD grabbed for the table and caught Olivia's laptop, as she had to save herself from a spill. "Sorry, kid. We're really taking it on the nose."

"I think I'm gonna be sick," Olivia said. Her hand waved off at the screen and she left the room to dive for the head across the passageway and inboard.

"Yikes."

"No joke," MD tentatively took the stool, then decided after a moment on the perch that he was better off standing. Something clattered on the deck above his head that sounded like a chair crashed into a desk after going on a ghost ride. "Little boat; big puddle. Do you know what you are doing next?"

"I can guess," Jason frowned. "Going hunting."

"It's why you have Charlie Company. The real reason. Do you have a plan?"

"We're packing up and heading south tomorrow," Jason said and held up a piece of paper. "Signed from both the state governor and the Homeland director ahead of time, just in case we found something close and needed to act. I'm also planning on bringing a detective with me. Our orders stated specifically that we were to backstop local law enforcement. If someone with a tin shield is out ahead of the charge, this means we are covered."

"I got all that," MD closed his eyes for a moment, willing his body to calm down. After a sharp exhale of breath, he continued. "Putting his name on the role we have been tracking, we can conclude that this Weatherly guy is an absolute psychopath. You know that moment of clarity and pause on the trigger before you drop someone? He doesn't have that check in his head from what we have seen, and he is likely out of control if he's been off doing all this stuff with no one knowing till now. That said, next steps? You have the stick. What is your plan?"

Jason gathered his thoughts. He'd made this call to get

advice for what to do with the data point Weatherly had offed the Godmother. Hunting was the obvious answer, and the order, or in this case, the suggestion he was hoping for. However, he hadn't thought it through. Now MD was asking him to do the planning, which Jason had hoped MD, Olivia, and Trevor would do for him.

Was this a turning point for me? A chance at something?

Still collecting himself, Jason looked over at the uniform top sitting on the bed with a captain's rank on the front Velcro, and remembered what that meant. Then he thought through what it felt like, three months ago, in the woods of Kentucky, for him and his friends to be hunted. To be critically wounded and then the flashes of memory of Brian and Molly tending to him, carrying him and protecting him all those miles.

"Since he wants to be heard, we focus on that. Here's what we are going to do..."

Chapter 21

Planning

"Was this a wise choice?" Molly asked, looking around the small clearing on the trail behind the hotel. Charlie company was falling in, some still in running gear having been caught out by the last minute change of schedule.

Jason was trying to look like he wasn't puffing from making the slightly sketchy wheeled assault on the rocky path up to this opening in the trees. He needed better tires or maybe a dog to tow him if he wanted to try anything deeper on trails. The mixed evergreen and oak forest around them smelled like pine and earth, although they were still close enough to the highway for the roar of tires and engines to filter through the leaves.

"Good morning, Company," Jason said. He spoke up, catching Timmons's eyes, and getting a nod back, confirming the bulk of the company was there. "Good dewy morning. We have arrived at the next step in this adventure. We are going hunting."

"The reason I dragged my broken ass up this trail was to honor an old tradition of battle planning on the sand. Also, the critter we are hunting has eyes and ears in places we can not trace, track, or mitigate at present. Raise your hand if you didn't follow the order of leaving electronic devices in your racks?"

No hands lifted under Jason's eyes as he swung them across all the short company.

"You all saw the building we were sent to investigate in Cambridge. You all helped sift the wreckage and recover what we could. To recap; a nasty varmint took out a United States Senator. Said critter has taken similar actions in the past. Our mission now is to stop him."

"Now, here's the problem. We have only a general idea where he may be, we have minimal intelligence, and I'm in a wheelchair. Oh, and we're not Marines."

The last brought some snickers.

"The benefit of the last is paramount to our plans, not because I don't trust Charlie Company to go charging into battle and slay; it's because we need to listen to what our enemy is telling us. See, Marines," Jason looked over at Molly, taking in her crossed arms, and cracking a smile towards her expression of general consternation. "Marines are superb at being pointed to a hill and taking that hill by sheer force of will. We are better at sitting back in the pocket, assessing, and then acting. We are the ones who are going to find that hill. Find, assess, and level if necessary and able."

"So that's what we are going to do. In the next few hours, we will sweep our vehicles for trackers, install some devices from RDI, and head down to begin a systematic sweep of a town on Cape Cod. Our target is likely living in or around Sandwich, Mass."

"Thanks to the efforts of Molly, and a tech from the DHS, we were able to track tolls, cameras and cell phone IDs down to Cape Cod. From there, some lucky metadata narrowed that search down to a few mile grid with a town code. Though it took half the night, I've leveraged a contact at NSA, and we have corroboration on those tracks and a few favors stored up for when we get stuck. We all work together. Each and every data point we add to the search parameters for the computer geeks at their desks is one more step to catching this guy. Anything you notice in the field, if you feel it's related; pass up the chain."

"Now," Jason paused. "Who here watched the news this morning?"

A few hands from those not in PT gear rose. Jason pointed around in one hand. "What was the message?"

"About the situation in Europe, or the gas leak in Boston?"

Jason shrugged. "Both. What did you hear? What did you feel?"

"That... Oh! That the tone shifted from the initial day when they called Boston a likely gas leak. This morning, they mentioned an expanding investigation into the explosion being malicious."

"But no mention of the word, terrorist, or specifically domestic terrorism."

"But that's what this is?" an older staff sergeant raised his hand. "Essentially. Right? An act of domestic terrorism?"

"Think on that for a moment," Jason patted his legs. "We are chasing a dude who ran, and potentially still runs, a shadow organization within a larger company which had access to the highest systems, persons and resources globally.

That's why no phones were allowed for this brief, and why the government sent you. Sent us. We are the sort of people who listen. When you go back to your morning, remember that. It's likely that someone will try to get information out of you. Notice it and report it up; we may need to use that phish event to misdirect. This is the key point. While we are about to go do some hunting, no one knows yet that we are heading in the right direction. No one, outside this circle, plus a few who are screening our efforts or supporting our logistics."

Jason checked his watch.

"See, right about now, three different news agencies just received word from the FBI that the investigation has shifted into the domestic terrorism multiple choice tick box. A joint task force is on their way along the I-90 turnpike towards Vermont to apprehend a convicted felon who was caught speeding with an expired inspection sticker the day of the explosion only a few miles from the location. Since we found tons of letters and irate voice messages from this person who used to work for our victim, at both of her houses as a contractor, the shoe fits."

"That is our distraction," Jason said coldly. "You will hear a name, Clarence Lareby. You will hear of some actions near Williamstown, MA. And you will probably see another explosion on the news. Don't worry, we didn't cause an innocent to get messed with. The identity is a cover, and since he's completed his investigation, spiking that identity with fire is just the system's way of sending him home from his task. We get the advantage of the sleight of hand."

"Because we are going south," Timmons said. "I always

wanted to go to Cape Cod."

"Correctly guessed. We are going south. Pack up, and fall out to the parking lot. Once outside, follow Molly's instructions. Each vehicle needs to be swept and then a care package installed. Don't worry, even Marines can follow the installation guide. Dismissed!"

"You are going to pay for that comment," Molly grumbled, walking past Jason's chair, and then lightly punching Brian in the arm as he had a grin like a ten-year-old who just watched his friend tag a runner out at first base.

It took a little over an hour to get the company all dialed in and augmented with the small BattleBoxes in each unit and better external antennas. Hoods pointed south, and they moved along like just any normal personnel transfer down to the expansive Cape Cod base for a summer exercise.

Chapter 22

In Range

"Uh, this is *Sandy Stewart* calling the *Crystal Dream*," Captain Bright opened Channel 16 on VHF after MD gave a nod. "Dream, you have ears on? You guys okay? We've been tracking you for a bit, and it looks like you got a sailor drunk at the helm. Did someone have too much of the tot?"

MD looked over Nori's shoulder at the tracking plot on the large monitor and grinned.

"Prankster," MD patted the younger man's shoulder. He pointed down at the ship's course track from breakfast time that morning when the Dream had been sideways to the wind for almost two hours. "That was downright mean."

"We hear ya, Stewart," Captain Santiago called back after a few moments. "While there's a bottle of 16-year-old Scotch locked in my desk, I am more than wishing I was halfway into it. We are having more than a small set of problems. Honestly, we hadn't noticed you were within twenty miles, or one of us would have warned you to stay clear."

"What seems to be the issue? From our plot, it looks like you may be stuck in fishing gear. Long line in your prop?

We're out a bit from normal pirate waters, but their snares can drift."

"I wish it were that simple," Santiago said. "We'd thought of that, but the bosun sent down a camera a few days ago and saw nothing. Since you're close, I'm considering asking if you can render aid. Critical subset of our issues is now two-fold. First, every time we try to make over five knots, something electrical screws up and the bow thruster tries to turn us sideways. We've been having an issue with our mains resetting, and the two seem to be related. Hours of troubleshooting phone calls to the manufacturer for support have gotten us nowhere. And second, and now more concerning, we lost our water desalinator this morning."

"Roger," Bright said. He smiled over at Nori and then set the hook. "I'd expect you to have a few weeks of water onboard. There should be plenty to get you back to port, even at five knots. Oh... I just did the math and checked the weather. Yikes! You may be in trouble with this storm."

"Ya, we can't outrun the typhoon coming down on us if we can only make five knots, and also, one of our two potable water tanks got backfilled by sewage this morning. The other tank transferred itself into the first while we were trying to fix things or some shit. If we can get the desal unit back up, we should be okay after we clean up stuff and change some pipes, but we're down to bottled water and sodas, and only have a few days on those without strict rationing. Since the sewage system is down... you get the picture. Every time we get ahead of one problem, another two crop up."

"What are you suggesting? Also, note *Dream* that we have three dive crews on board with full underwater salvage gear to back them up."

"Let me think on this for a few, but how would you feel about taking a personnel transfer?"

"We are tight, but have plenty of supplies. Might as well make this official. Are you calling it? If not, we really shouldn't hang out for very long. I really don't want to leave you guys in the way of a storm without rudder control."

"Agreed." Santiago took a deep breath. "PANPAN PAN-PAN PANPAN! This is *Crystal Dream* calling PANPAN PAN-PAN. Vessel in distress because of inability to navigate and in need of assistance. Souls on board thirty-three. Vessel calling, *Sandy Stewart*, could you take a transfer of thirteen? Science party, plus two of our crew with minor injuries."

"We can do so. Also note, we have heavy capstan and recovery gear. I don't like the concept of doing a personnel transfer under way with you out of control, and we just caught something on sonar in your wake down about 300 meters. I think you're hooked up on a shot of chain, *Dream!*"

"Wish to rig us up for a tow? Also, if you get us out of this mess, that bottle of Scotch is yours!"

"For safety, I'd prefer to rig you in tow for sure. As we are now starboard of your wake, I'm going to keep us to this side of whatever you might drag behind you, and swing wide. We'll gear up to put divers in the water and see if you're caught up in a long line. One RHIB will pass up a line you can use to haul back a wire rope. Once we get you stable, we'll send over some water and take your people. Sounds good?"

"It would be a relief!"

"No time like the present," Captain Bright spoke over his

shoulder to Nori.

The man pressed the spacebar on his laptop, leaned back in his chair and jauntily put his hands on the back of his head to prepare for admiring his work.

"Crap, Stewart," Santiago called over VHF. "We just had a fire light off in our incinerator room! I'm putting our science party in Gumby suits and getting them ready on the main deck, starboard amidships."

"We see a black plume on your 02, port side," Bright said. He lowered his binoculars and gave Nori a thumbs-up. "We'll have boats in the water in five! Also, a pair of inspection drones will be on the way. They have thermals."

The idea of staging a fire had been the *Stewart's* bosun, backed up by Bright as an alternative to the original idea of splashing down some decks with slippery fluid. Since having most of the crew in a spot or two was the fastest way to secure the ship, the best path to do that was to mock a fire.

"Good sell, Captain," MD said, tossed the strap of his AR10 over his shoulder and headed for the ladder.

"When they figure out all I did was close the air damper too far and make it smoke and then trigger the temp warning, they may be miffed."

"Oh, Mister Hong, I think they are about to be miffed by more than just having to drag their fire gear around the ship for no reason," Bright nodded to the first officer at the helm. "As soon as the last boat's away, get us to starboard one kilometer and then burn north to come even with them. Nori, are you sure you can keep them stable as soon as we make contact? No need to actually hook to them? Towing at sea is serious business."

"Yes, captain," Nori said. He took one moment to read over the script on his screen and nod. "It's laid in. I've been slowly bringing them around into the wind so they don't notice, and will lock in that heading and speed. While they have messed with a few things, and tried a few software patches; we're still in control."

*****

"Damn it to hell!"

Santiago looked over at the AB Doug, who was halfway into the bunker gear in the lockers just aft of the bridge. The first mate was right behind him, already snugging up the fasteners on his boots before grabbing the thick suspenders. The cook had just called out on their radios that the science party was ignoring her commands.

"Doug, you're more intimidating. Go straight to the lab deck machine shop and make those idiots get in their immersion suits and move to their muster station. If we have to abandon ship, they need to be ready!"

"This should be fun," Doug snapped the fasteners closed on his jacket and dumped the SCBA gear over his head.

Hat on head, mask dangling at the ready, Doug took the ladder downward three to five steps at a time until he hit the main deck. Passing two fire doors forward, he banged on the lab door and one of the armed guards opened it.

Once inside, the large project lead, whose face was redder than ever, charged Doug.

"What is going on? We have to work!" Sydney Brenner growled. "We can't keep getting interrupted by bullshit!"

Doug didn't flinch at the approaching man, who was oblivious to the flashing fire alarm strobe lights. Taking two handfuls of the man's shirt, he dragged the guy closer.

"Get your team into their survival suits! Get to the hanger! Do it now, or we will begin dragging you out."

"What is happening?" a woman in a white lab coat asked shakily, an orange suit bag in her hands.

The AB shoved Brenner back into a counter. He then stomped over to the scared woman, grabbed the bag from her and expertly yanked it in the air, which snapped open the fasteners and dumped out the red-orange three-fingered "Gumby" immersion suit onto the deck.

"We are on fire." Dough emphasized each word, then pointed to the cook, a short but broad woman with a clipboard in her hands who stood near the locker of suits with a radio on her vest. "Follow her instructions or you could die. Clear!?!"

Orange bags were opened and the cook began helping an older man, a machinist, get to the deck and get his boots off.

The AB turned to the four men with rifles and vests who had clumped together after he entered. "I'd recommend you guys ditch that armor and grab a suit. Or at least be ready to do so."

Two exchanged glances, faces grim, but the lead shook his head.

"We stay here till we can't. Don't worry about us. We know what to do, and won't get in your way."

Throwing up his hands, and then shaking his head at Brenner, who was still fuming mad, Doug slammed out of the door, dogged the hatch and took off at a run for the nearest ladder up to the 02.

Chapter 23

Boarding

Olivia held her gear at the ready and gave a knife hand to starboard, made the sign to show she had one shot to make, and then shouldered her SCAR-H battle rifle. One leg locked into a rope loop and the opposite arm locked to another. She stabilized for Williams to cut their RHIB around over a swell and then turn into the port side of the Dream.

The maneuver gave her less than two seconds to line up the shot on the armed man on the exterior 02 deck on the forward quarter. As the RHIB smoothly rolled off the back side of the wave, the soldier saw their boat, spotted the rifle, noted it was pointed at him, and then dropped as the two shots Olivia squeezed off arrived.

The boat kicked up to full throttle, and a pair of drones launched off the rear platform with boarding lines. Entirely handled thanks to a BattleBox plugin, no human interaction was needed for the next steps. The software had no issues trailing the line systems safely over their heads to its mark on the rail of the 03 deck, just above where the man Olivia shot lay dead on the salt coated steel.

In thirty seconds, Fred Stone, Ivan and two of the Seals rode the lines up through their battery powered hoists. Olivia and Randy followed. The group paired off as trained and went door to door, half going forward and half aft. In less than three minutes, they had the deck cleared and entered the space outside the incinerator, where most of the crew were preparing to fight the simulated "fire" event.

Only one noticed their entry and had the mind to react. The large Doug swung a breaching tool at Ivan, but the far bigger RDI contractor simply caught it, dragged the AB forward, and twisted while Fred Stone kicked the legs out from under Doug, who was already top heavy with the air tank and bunker gear.

Their team zip-tied the crew to handrails with the heavy gear, making any act of fighting almost impossible. Radios were stripped and tossed in a trash bag.

"Fire team neutralized," Olivia called out on their secure comms. "Feel free and kill the smoke, Stewart Ops."

"On it."

"Okay," Olivia nodded to the Seals. "You two keep them honest. Let's find the others."

*****

As MD's RHIB came up on the starboard side, a pair of drones buzzed past them.

"That was close," he said. His words vanished uselessly into the wind.

"WHAT!" Fat Al shouted back.

"NOTHING!"

MD knife-handed to their spot, and the cox cut in at full throttle to kiss the rubber against steel.

One seal with them deftly shouldered a launcher, and a ladder flew up and locked onto their target.

Fat Al was reaching for the ladder when the dull double thump of rounds from the opposite side of the ship could be heard. That didn't make him hesitate, but he did duck to the hull at a call and answer of automatic fire above their heads.

"Two down," Petty Officer Smith said. Her words cut through the noise via comms from the Stewart. "They tried to shoot one drone."

Just before Al could make another grab at the ladder, a shot from the RHIB behind them cracked out.

"One down, just outside the hangar," Trevor called out.

"GO," said MD. He spanked Fat Al, and the man reached up, captured a rung and began hauling.

MD followed, barely able to keep up with the younger guy on his still shaky leg. Once on the 02, they ignored the inner hatch, checked the two bodies that the drones had shot down, and then sprinted on the slippery deck for the exterior ladder up to the bridge.

On making entry, the team fanned out around the raised hands of the captain. MD prepared to approach Santiago, but caught a hint of movement to his left and down the ladder inside. Seeing a barrel pass the threshold, he raised, and then fired at the armed man coming up around.

A single shot rang back up the passageway and Fat Al cried out and dropped to a knee. MD finished the man down the ladder with three more quick shots. A Seal pushed past while he covered to check the body and take up a position on the door.

In the exchange, Santiago made a dive for a handheld

radio in a cup holder. Cynthia caught his ankle with her foot, yanked, and sent the man to land face first on the deck before he made it halfway.

"All clear?" MD asked.

"I think I'll stay here," the Seal called from down the ladder, mounted up in the door to the next deck.

"Got 'em covered," the second RDI New Mexico teammate said.

The last three posted up on the two outside ladders to watch the decks.

"You good?" MD moved towards Al, who had pulled a trauma bandage out of his FAK and was holding his rear.

Making eye contact, MD didn't hesitate in saying the words.

"This is where I have to tell you to bend over." MD tapped Al's arm and then his bloody hand, taking over the pressure.

"Fine! I don't think it's too bad. Bounced off the wall." Al dropped his rifle into one of the deck mounted chairs and grabbed the back with his hands.

Flashlight out, MD removed the bandage, probed a little, cut away half a butt cheek of pants with a pair of EMT shears. The leaking slash had an obvious solution. He pressed on both sides of the wound while yanking out a piece of full metal jacket with his multi-tool.

"It'll need stitches, but you're fine."

MD slapped a bandage on the wound to seal it temporarily, which caused a hiss to emerge.

"Thanks," Al laughed and quoted from the mission briefings. "Beware bouncers. Shot in the ass by one. Figures."

"Good thing you already have a nickname," Seal 2 leader

said. "Clear here, sir."

MD remembered his situation and did what he should have, keying up his comms.

"Bridge clear. One down. One captured. On injured. Stable on mission."

*****

Trevor didn't let himself get distracted by the gunfire forward. He had his sights locked on a lone man with a rifle who had just ducked into the hangar on the main deck. When the man poked his head back out to look towards MD's RHIB, Trevor let fly a shot. It struck the man in the shoulder, but the form dove for the deck, likely still in play.

His RHIB moved in to make for the escape ladder the crew of the Dream had dropped over the side to facilitate a transfer and Trevor monitored the rail with Collin next to him, scanning aft, and a Seal watching forward. A smattering of fire struck the water behind them and then a crack of rifle round zinging through the air came well over their heads.

Following the stout zing, a body fell through the opening in the rail, and Trevor ducked back. Collin, who had been looking far down the main deck towards the other end of the hangar, wasn't as fortunate and had no time to react to get out of the way. The large body, spewing gore the way only a 50 BMG impact can quite accomplish, slammed into him from the 30 ft drop and knocked him out of the RHIB.

"One down." Michael confirmed over the comms.

"Man in the water! Starboard amidships!" Damion announced, stomping on Michael's message.

The Seal driving Trevor's RHIB yelled something resembling "HOLD ON!" and everyone got low and grabbed ropes.

With a snarl from the engine, the RHIB bounced off the hull, cut around to starboard, made a harrowing twisty dance on the next wave, and cut in on Collin. The coxswain deftly dumped speed and feathered the boat into reverse to allow Trevor to loop his arm into Collin's over the side. As the next wave crashed in, Trevor and the Seal team lead hauled the man onboard.

The maneuver in this sea state caused the tail of the RHIB to take on some wash. The engine sputtered, coughed, cackled a few times; died, and then restarted. And then the craft was sideways at carefully delivered power once more on the front edge of a wave and heading back to the Dream.

In the pause for the recovery, the fourth RHIB led by Sam had taken their spot in the stack and started their boarding.

"Man recovered," Damion confirmed on comms from his perch on the Stewart.

"You good?" Trevor asked Collin, who was trying to deflate the automatic horseshoe shaped inflatable life vest he had on under his body armor.

"That hurt," Collin said, wiping blood off of his face and neck. Some of it was his, most though likely the man who struck him even after the brief bath. When the wipe of blood had to be repeated, he frowned. "What the hell?"

Trevor turned Collin's face, watched the seeping for a moment and debated between quick-clot or sealer.

"I think you got a road rash from the hand guard on that dude's rifle. The spacing is a straight up Picatinny rail imprint."

Collin accepted a can of sealer, sprayed himself and nodded at the ship. The other RHIB had just pulled off to clear the ladder.

"I'm good. Let's go!"

*****

Sam saw Collin flop overboard with the body drop from the sky and knifed her hand in.

"GO, we take their space!"

With a roar of the motor, the fourth RHIB cut past the turning craft, trying to recover Collin and slapped the metal of the Dream. Sam let one seal grab the ladder first, as she wasn't as confident in leading a charge. Rifles carefully cycled from a scan of rails to sling and climb.

What she found in the hangar disturbed her. They expected thirteen people, and there were indeed thirteen in the hangar. Six men, and seven women. One large man was struggling into a Gumby suit. She didn't think he'd finish making it in, but he raised his eyes to her and they were full of challenge.

"I'm Brenner!" he said. The announcement triggered a huff to catch his breath. "Get us out of here and you will be well paid! Also, I need someone to get my cat out of my cabin."

Sam kicked him away from her with a solid teep to his nuts.

"PO Secure this man!" Sam said. Once the Seal Petty Officer next to her had a hand on Brenner, she moved her attention to the rest of the party. "Anyone have injuries?"

Two women raised their hands. Sam checked over the hangar, noted that the mixed RDI New Mexico team and seals had already moved to cover the entrances on the main deck. Moving to the first woman who had a hand up, the smell of ... excrement and vinegar emanating from her almost overcame Sam.

"What happened?"

The stinky woman, her long black hair stringy and caked with grime and grease, wasn't all the way tucked into her hood. She held up her left arm. "Crushed by a pipe."

Sam touched the three-fingered integrated suit glove gently with one hand and probed down with her other. Half way, the wincing and pull away made it obvious. "Ulna fracture."

"Was thinking the same," the woman said. "It's taped up. Not through the skin."

Sam waved for Brian Honeysuckle to come over with his heavier medical bag and unzipped the woman's suit. She backed away at both the smell and the need to check on the other injured woman.

The second female shied away from the touch at her hood. Shaking her head, the small Asian woman pulled away further.

"It's okay honey, what's your injury? Nothing's going to happen to you, girl."

The woman pointed down to her belly. Sam raised an eyebrow and then gasped as a rifle round took her in the back. She dropped to cover the girl as more rounds stitched into her rear plate.

Answering fire from the Seal kicked off, and Sam raised her head up from its tucked state to respond. Even with ear protection on, the sudden crack and echo of gunfire in the large metal hangar jarred the senses. The science party, without headgear on, all ducked and covered.

"Shit," the PO said, nodding up an almost hidden ladder inside the hangar at a flapping door at the forward wall. "Didn't get em, captain. You good?"

Sam got to her feet, rifle back up and on the open door, forcing her lungs to shrug off the effects of the impacts on her back. "I'm good. Vest caught it. Anyone else hit?"

She turned to see Brian Honeysuckle's body laying over the woman whom he'd been halfway through, bracing her broken arm. To add insult to injury, the large man was now bleeding out on top of her, with her arms flailing around in a panic.

"Someone help them!" Sam ordered and charged up the ladder with a nod at the Seal. On comms, she called. "Brian's down in the hangar. We have a runner on the 01 with a rifle! Heading forward from the main hangar!"

*****

Olivia heard the call, tapped Fred on the shoulder, and then tore off towards the bow of the ship.

Sliding to a stop at the end of the passage, she gently opened a hatch on the starboard side, dogged the door behind her, thankful that the crew had greased the latches, and stepped gently forward to view the front deck area. She spotted a shadow in the low light crouched behind one of the lifeboat stands on the port side. Rather than find a way down inside, Olivia cradled her rifle, dove off the rail, and dropped the fifteen feet in a roll to the deck.

She snapped back up from her roll into a sprint and fired off one round as she aligned with the man hiding. Her round struck the lifeboat case. Return fire bounced off of the deck behind her, but she kept on her sprint all the way to slam into the man with a knee strike to his midsection. Following with a slap to the hand which held an iridium phone, she was satisfied by seeing the electronic device sail over the rail and into the dark, and a short-barreled M4 clone spin out of his hands to slide across the deck.

A strong shove from the larger form knocked her back several feet. Unwilling to let the space stay, she closed again, smacked her elbow down on the arm which was drawing a pistol from a holster, and then spun and fired her other elbow directly at the man's face. He caught it in guard, tried to make space again, and then had to deal with the fact that her clinch allowed all the leverage she needed to drive her left knee into his crotch. Twice.

The man dropped to the deck but hung her up on the way and brought her down with him. A flash of steel in the end of daylight was all the warning she needed to dive into her best effort at a full lock as she took the man's back.

While she received a deep slash on her leg in the process of locking up the man, they were now in a final battle. He wanted to get the blade arm free; she wanted that blade to cut his head off. Since she could feel the form of his armor against her chest and arms, she had a limited set of options to end this exchange, as he was a skilled fighter and almost twice her size.

Leveraging all of her hard earned extra core strength, paid for by her daily swims for the last few months, and using every moment of her thirteen years of gymnastics competition and all the painful lessons learned in martial arts training for twice that time, Olivia picked a path. With a scream heard all the way to the decks of the Stewart, Olivia bridged, twisted, shifted her leg lock to the left side, and then levered her soul into driving the captured fixed blade under the man's left armpit and deep into his chest.

"Fuck. You." Olivia hissed, keeping pressure on the fighter as he bled out and eventually stilled. The distinct iron, coppery scent of pooling blood mixed with the salt spray as the sun finished setting on the stormy horizon.

Chapter 24

Lost

"Look, you know we are tasked with finding a phone. And we have permission to look for it in any data set. I thought we had this all cleared and covered. Do I need to get Charlotte on the phone, Carl? Again? Did the NSA forget the memo?" Jason shook his head and set it down in his hands.

After a breath, he glanced back up at his cell phone, which was sitting in the cup holder with a video chat on. Said cup holder was not standard equipment for a Humvee. Some helpful national guardsman had clipped it into a crack in the dash. It had then been taped, glued, and taped again over the years. It was handy.

"It's not like we are asking you to give us an identity or anything. You have the location information, obviously. We do not."

"Jason, it's not about that," Carl Harding frowned into the camera. "Hang on. Let me see if I can figure out another way of helping you. Jason, you know I'm very limited in what I can do."

"All the state law enforcement data showed our target

phone was in Sandwich. The FBI searches showed Sandwich. The Homeland query we ran showed the same. But it's not here. We've checked every tower in the zip code more than once."

"That's because it's in Mashpee," Carl said. The man frowned, closed his eyes, scrunched up his face at his accidental leak, and looked down. After he recovered his composure, he added a quick phrase to cover his mistake. "The best pizza, that is. Try out the pizza in Mashpee and let me know what you think? I've gotta drop. I hope you have a wonderful dinner."

Jason stared at his phone for a few moments and then looked over at the determined, but exhausted Molly, who was standing in his open door. She pulled up a map of the nearby town on her phone and searched through the app for pizza places. "There's a gas station.... Dino's and then one restaurant in the shopping center which sells wood-fired pizza. Dino's has 4.5 stars. The others are rather poorly rated."

"It's 4 PM," Jason checked the website for the Dino's, read through the menu, and grinned. "Timmons, can you call a contact and get someone to find us some bunks at Camp Edwards, in Bourne? We should have probably done that call hours ago. My bad."

"I can try, sir," the man added a modern correction. "It's called the Joint Base Cape Cod now."

"Exactly; Camp Edwards." Jason ignored the update and made a phone call.

"Yes... I've got a bunch of hungry Army down on cape with me, and my navigator missed a turn to Camp Edwards. Any chance I can order 30... No, better make that 35 pizzas for my boys? Ya... we took a wrong turn off of the rotary or something. Traffic was a pissah... Okay... Let's go with ten pepperoni, ten house specials, and five mushrooms. Man, those look good. Five buffalo chicken, and five vegetarians. Oh, and can you also add in like eighty hot wings? Extra blue cheese."

Molly lightly thumped Jason's shoulder and mouthed the word: *SALAD*!

"And also, add in five steak tip salads; balsamic vinai-grette on the side... Awesome! We will be there... Nice, thanks for the info. We'll park on the side lot. No worries. Can I give you my card now?"

Jason completed the large order with his RDI American Express and added a 25% tip on the phone.

"Well," Molly sniffed from the door. "Happy with your-self?"

Jason held up the map on his phone with a circuitous route any poor corporal might accidentally tap into their GPS taking a convoy just like theirs on the wrong path, going to MA-6 instead of keeping on Route 3, and then back on Highway 401 right past Dino's Sports Bar.

"Timmons?" Molly asked. "What time is chow, normally on bases?"

"Really depends, but I'd expect... Since this is a mixed base, done by 1730."

"I..." Molly paused. "Oh. Ya, the traffic. There's no way we'd make it, get checked in and stuff and have a chance of cycling through. Okay, I retract my point. The MREs you guys brought give Brian gas."

"I have a point, though," Brian said softly from the back

seat. He had his eyes closed for a bit of the initial conversation, but he appeared completely awake instantly.

"Is it whether you should eat a salad?" Molly crossed her arms.

Holding up a hand towards Molly, but turning that hand to a thumbs-up, he spoke slowly. "How much do you trust your NSA spook, Carl?"

"That's a good question," Timmons backed up Brian and lowered his phone. "Their steak tips look good, but seriously? We have blown a bunch of fuel today, and us driving around with the core group parked in a rest stop a few miles up the road has likely been noticed. Do you trust this intel? Not saying we don't eat some dinner. We have to be cautious here."

"I trust Carl," Jason nodded. "I think he made a mistake by letting the location slip. He's a solid resource. Bit of a stick up his ass about rules, but there are reasons for that. They have tight leashes, and the oversight is bonkers. He spends half of his time filling out permission slips to log into servers, or even sometimes to read an email a second time."

"Okay." Timmons swiped through some text messages. "And upside is, the Joint Base can pass us an entire barracks building normally for the Coast Guard who come up here for cold weather training and stuff. We have digs for the night. And it has AC, too, unlike many of the older structures."

At the delayed response from Jason, Timmons almost commented. Noticing how focused both Jason and Molly were on their phones, he let them complete their flow.

"Only four cell phone towers," Molly tapped and then looked up.

"Maybe five," Jason showed his feed to her, with a marker dropped on a hill far to the west, near MA-3.

Molly shrugged. "That one might be in range. Maybe if you were on a hill or climbed a tree. Either way, we should be able to get a good bit of data while parked near the pizza place. I'd leave a BattleBox there when we head to base."

"Lets collect everyone and get on it, then. Food awaits!"

Chapter 25

Breakfast

"I will add this to the retrospective," Olivia frowned, but pointed to her chest. "This was my fault. We didn't properly account because running two ships without a second crew for this one was short sighted. Having a spare prize crew with us would have been a good idea. That said, we've completed our initial taking with some losses."

"Clarify those losses, if you would?" Berger asked on the call.

"Brian Honeysuckle, our team medic, was killed. Three of us were injured in the assault. Just bumps and stitches. Also, we could only apprehend one of the ten security forces aboard the ship, General. All the other nine members of the security detail guarding the nuclear weapons manufacturing facility were killed in the initial minutes of the action."

"Thank you, Ms. Kuznetsov," Berger frowned. "Taking a ship with minimal intel ahead of time is always a gamble. I'm sorry your team suffered a loss."

"Wouldn't have been possible without your support. I appreciate the thanks, General," Olivia said. She almost made a comment about how the bastard who killed Brian Honeysuckle while the man was literally trying to set a young woman's broken arm had been avenged. The thought turned sour in her mouth. "Are you aware of what our plans are for the Crystal Dream?"

"How can we be sure you have extracted all useful intelligence from the ship?" Jones asked.

Olivia smiled sincerely. "Well, Mr. Jones, that we are providing you with the entire complement of staff who ran the facility. Not to mention pictures of everything. All the components, the stores of almost forty completed W82 nuclear warheads, and proof of a storage locker containing three sample detonator cores; I would hope that stands for something resembling a complete useful resource set."

"It ... does," Jones began, but General Berger interrupted.

"Our missing member would speak up about that," Berger said. "She would say several things at this point about the next steps we should take. While preserving this evidence is at some level important; what is the point? I also remind the committee that the RDI charter is very clear in situations like this. They are under an obligation to destroy this vessel as it sits; not just because it is a hazard to navigation, as its control systems are not intact, not because it has a substantial stockpile of material necessary to make nuclear weapons, but simply because it exists. Bad people know about it, and they also know this precious resource is likely in a vulnerable condition. The simplest path for all involved is to scuttle this ship where it is."

"Upside is," Olivia added. "A typhoon is already on our proverbial doorstep. Public tracking systems have shown this ship has been having profound issues navigating, spanning back months. And as we will be at max speed, dealing with the weather from said typhoon, it is a huge safety risk to all remaining lives from both ships to tow the vessel clear of the weather."

"I'm sorry to still object a bit to this." Jones scrunched up his face in a brief show of frustration. "Getting some of our agents onboard would go a long way to ease our concerns of something important being missed."

"You just mean," the usually silent and bored DHS representative spoke up, which required a clearing of the throat to continue. "You just really mean you'd love to get your hands on a bunch of untracked weapons."

"As I lead you back to Berger's reminder; RDI has a charter which establishes very specific standards. We also have a responsibility to honor maritime law. And we are more than ready, willing and able to deliver the entire crew and every scrap of electronics recovered from this ship to whichever port this committee requests. Allowing this ship to run derelict is not an option given the sea conditions. Repairing the damage done to the water and sewage systems isn't something we have the resources to complete before the storm. And we do not know if another party may be on the way to take it back. It needs to disappear."

Jones opened his mouth as if to say something and then closed it and looked over to Berger who was sitting next to him in the camera feed.

"Unless there are objections?" Berger switched to a formal syntax. "I am proposing for this committee to release RDI to complete their task to their standard. Delivery of all acquired personnel and assets is further requested to be performed at the port of Guam, at best speed able given the deteriorating weather condition in the region. Electronic data dumps of any audio and video recorded during the entire operation to be delivered without edit within three months' time."

"All in favor?"

Most of the virtual hands raised, and Jones snuck his hand into the air.

"Any opposed?"

General Berger waited several seconds, but saw no hits.

"Motion masses. Olivia Kuznetsov, RDI mission lead, you are authorized to take the actions you see fit relating to the disposition of the Crystal Dream. Please provide this committee with an estimated time of arrival of persons in Guam as soon as you can."

"Thank you. We will do as we need to comply. Out here, then." Olivia signed, and killed the feed. She looked over her laptop at Trevor, Team X lead, and MD who were listening along on the opposite wall. "Any issues with that?"

"None." Trevor said. He snickered, then backpedaled with a snort. "Well, one. I hate Guam."

The Seal team lead, Chief Petty Officer Miller, just turned and waved over his shoulder as this stuff was all outside his wheelhouse. Sam shrugged, and that left... MD.

He looked Olivia in the eye, checked a feed on his phone, and then radioed the bridge who was waiting for this call. "Bridge, Lab. Are we at least 5 nautical miles away from the ship?"

"Yes, Lab, this is Bridge. We are currently almost 11 miles from the Crystal Dream."

MD passed Olivia a detonator fob, which would relay through their onboard systems to the underwater ACOMMS for almost 20 miles. "It's yours to kill."

Olivia accepted the device, nodded to the room, and then keyed up the comms to the bridge.

"Bridge, Lab. We are prepared to start scuttle charges. Are we clear to do so at this time?"

"Send it, Lab." Captain Bright said. "Scope is clear. Range hot."

"Notice; charges firing on our shadow companion in 3... 2... 1... Mark."

At the press of the button, a sequence of specially made scuttling charges essentially unzipped the welds on the keel of the Crystal Dream. With almost every lower compartment and ladder up to the top decks suddenly open to the sea, the ship quickly dropped into the dark. On its way down, a programmed sequence of secondary charges had been set to fire at specific depths, which would be nearly undetectable or unnoticed by any potential observer in the air. When the wreck passed 200 meters depth, a 500 pound Russian sourced scuttle charge exploded in an intentionally sealed space of the machine shop to shred the tooling systems and jigs. Passing 800 meters, the substantially shielded shipping container in the hold containing the completed W82 warheads detonated, using one of the three discovered initiators, plus a trigger Collin installed. The single boosted 2 kiloton explosion took out the rest of the warheads, the nearby storage locker of materials to make more, and completed rendering anything in the ship of remote value into essentially unrecoverable scrap.

While the others left the small lab space after a few minutes, Olivia stayed to watch the sonar plot until the trace of the main body of the wreck touched the ocean floor at just over 7100 meters, almost two hours later. Brenner's cat was her companion for that duty; staying on her lap the entire time.

"Message sent." Olivia scratched the cat behind her ears. "What was this turkey feeding you? Let's go find you some meat."

Chapter 26

Solutions

"The steak tips were surprisingly good."

Brian walked over to the room tagged for Molly and a female sergeant from ODA 3430. Tossing her bag in, he crossed and sat down at the large table in the center of 12 2-person rooms. Timmons was looking over Molly's shoulder at her laptop and he had a paper map of the base out in his hands, folded to one far corner, which was the subject of their attention.

Molly looked up and glared at Brian as he snagged a piece of pizza from one box of leftovers. "You sure? Might regret that."

The man contemplated the piece for a few moments, shrugged and then began to decimate it.

"Isn't that like your fourth?"

"Second," Brian mumbled, halfway through a bite.

Jason returned from tossing the empty salad tray and a coke can in the trash. "I think if I lived near here. I'd crush Dino's all the time. Solid. Cheap too."

"And since anyone nearby would frequent it, of course, is

why we left a BattleBox there," Molly said. She compared the map on her screen to the map in Timmons's hand one more time. "You guys sure we are given full access? We can go anywhere on base property. Right?"

"We have permission," Jason said. He nodded to Timmons, collected one of the empty pizza boxes, and trashed it. "With a few call-first-verify-before locations marked by signage."

"You know, that's what the corporals we brought from admin are supposed to be in charge of, sir," Timmons teased. "Throwing out the trash. No captain should bus his own boxes. You gotta get with the program, sir."

"Speaking of bussing boxes," Molly said. She dropped her finger to a point on the base map slightly northwest of Dino's, on the other side of a pond. "I'd like to get a BattleBox there. Right now, if possible. Before it gets too much later in the evening."

"I'm good with that," Jason yawned. "Timmons, you good?"

The man snorted a response, passed Molly the map and grabbed the last slice of a House Special from a box and stuck it in his mouth.

Jason wheeled over next to Molly. "Even though we're on base, take two squads. While he's getting people ready, walk me through it. What do you have over in that corner?"

Molly pointed to her screen with one hand and the base map with her other. "This campground and beach at the edge of the lake north of Dino's has a trail, I believe, originally just a fire road, that snakes right up to and then follows the edge of the base for a few miles over to this road. Issue is, this road's not on Google Maps properly, or it's not on the base map properly. Something's just... off. I want to go look, and while there, drop a box at this gate."

Switching to a topographical map, Molly frowned. "See, something's just not right."

"Agreed," Jason said, noticing the discrepancy. "This far out in the sticks, though? Could just be a simple mistake. Looks to be very few houses on that road."

"Ready when you are," Timmons said, his head poked through the door. "Taking four Humvees. You okay with that, captain?"

"Oh, now you're honoring the stripes?" Jason asked. He waved a hand in apology as Timmons struck a pose and put a fake hurt expression on his face. "Ya, no reason to rock an MRAP around."

"I would have brought an MRAP, but they're all getting fueled at the moment. Those things are hungry bastards, and there's a line ahead of us thanks to some Air Force taser training or potato launching event."

Molly packed up her bag and then noticed Jason wasn't moving. "Not coming?"

Jason shook his head. "Nooooo. Nuh uh... I've been bent over for too long. If I don't stretch out and do some PT, I'm gonna be useless tomorrow."

Brian passed Molly her rifle and waved for the door.

It took them a while to snake to the far corner of the base from their billet near Bourne, MA. At just under 22,000 acres, the facility which absorbed Otis plus Camp Edwards and now included five military commands took up a large portion of Upper Cape Cod.

Brian passed the time by scrolling through random news feeds on his phone with one ear bud in. Fighting the urge to yawn and wishing she had some coffee, Molly drew out her laptop when they got close to the Mashpee fence line. Viewing the logs from the local towers, she almost immediately understood what had happened with their initial confusion over which town to hunt.

"The towers are ... tagged wrong." Molly laughed. "On one system, the locations are accurate. On the other, it's reporting the Mashpee towers as Sandwich towers. That has to explain the original confusion."

Brian tapped into his location app from the back seat and nodded. "The interweb says we are in Sandwich."

"But we're on base, so technically in neither town, and we are WAY far from Sandwich. The town ends almost fifteen miles west of us. There's so few cell phones hitting these towers, likely no one noticed or cared. Locals know where they are, so what's the point in fixing things? I think it was just a goof. They paved over an old road called Sandwich Road and failed to program in the right zip code or town name somewhere along the line when cell towers kicked online."

Timmons had a Corporal Brown driving and tapped the young man on the shoulder to turn off towards an access road on the right. The entire section of the base they had been driving on for the last twenty minutes was simply unused. This broad access road could take four semi trucks side by side with wiggle room. Based on the banking and drainage work on either side, it had both been there for a while, and seen little use recently other than lawn mowing semiannually.

"From the base 2ic, this area was carved out as a potential

space port in the late 70s, to be put into place in the 80s if the situation warranted it. Other than maintenance, and some infrastructure projects to ensure water and natural gas were available for some of the other parts of the base, it's been unused by anything other than deer and coyotes."

"You realize we just passed a pair of missile silos?" Brian glanced over his shoulder, struggling to take a picture with his camera.

Molly shuddered and then pointed off to the left. "Down that fire road is the cell tower. Let's go all the way to the gate, though. I want to see what this public road looks like outside the base. It connects directly back into the neighborhoods behind Dino's past Johns Pond and the campground."

Over one small hill, they spotted the base gate. A guard house held the center of the large intersection. It was in good repair, but obviously out of recent use. One lane of the broad paved entrance way was blocked by concrete blocks roped together with heavy cable, and the other had a long gate chained to a stout steel framework.

"Any chance you can get us the combo?" Molly asked, getting out and walking over to the guard post. She frowned as the power wasn't switched on, but the BattleBox would be good for a day on its own. Switching the unit into "deploy" mode, she stood on the bench and raised it up to set it on a rafter.

Almost dropping the box as a few hornets began buzzing around, she squeaked, pushed it in one more inch and dove outside. Her heart thumped as two of the angry insects gave up the brief chase with the distance.

Timmons shook his head. "Whew! Those are bald faced

hornets. Nasty little bastards. The commander's office is working on the combo for the gate lock. May take a minute, given the hour."

Molly looked up and down the recently repaved Sandwich Road that ran along the outside of the south edge of the base. Some time in the last few years, a sidewalk had been constructed on the opposite side. The rolling hills of this section didn't allow for much visibility. She looked to the east, back towards Mashpee, thinking about how the trails led back past the lake. A man in running shorts with a day pack was paused with hands on hips, panting on the sidewalk. He reached into the pack for a water bottle and then she saw him open up his phone as if checking his lap time or changing the track on a playlist.

Her phone vibrated, and she froze. Molly began walking towards the road, ducking under the gate. She checked her phone, read the notification from the alert system on the BattleBox feeds, and then she moved her rifle around to her front and ran.

"Weatherly?!"

At the call of the name, the man turned and then started fumbling in his day pack while shuffling backwards in surprise. At the glint of steel, Molly raised her rifle, debating at the last moment where to place the shot. Thinking back to Jason in the chair, recovering from taking five rounds through his pelvis, she aimed for the bowl. A crack from Weatherly's pistol rang out and Molly squeezed off a round in response.

At the direct hit to his pubic bone, the man crumpled in place like a bag of rags, pistol fumbled into the ditch and a bottle of water rolled away onto the road. Brian and Timmons were past her in a second, both sprinting with rifles raised. A roar of engine and a crash of metal announced the Humvees breaking through the gate and heading their way.

"One down," Brian called over comms while ripping his blowout kit off his pack.

Timmons had his phone out, and a fire team poured from the lead Humvee, which blocked them to the east, and the tail covered to the west. "Ya, 911, this is Master Sergeant Timmons, United States Army. We are just outside of JBCC Unified Base Gate 1741 on Sandwich Road, about midway between the Masphee line and the next crossroad. Gunshot victim in need of immediate medical assistance. I would... consider sending a life flight. He is..."

Brian waved a bloody gloved hand over his shoulder and shook his head.

"One sec," Timmons looked down, noting Brian had switched from trying to stop the massive bleeding to checking for a pulse, and then beginning CPR. A sergeant from ODA3433 was shoving packing material in the hole as fast as she could. With the amount of blood on the ground and obvious internal bleeding because of the location of the entry wound and nasty exit fragmentation, it didn't look like it was going to be worth the effort. "Just send a bus. No pulse, likely arterial hit in the pelvis. We are performing CPR. Doubt he's going to make it."

Molly leaned down, picked up Weatherly's cell phone and swiped the screen. It was still unlocked.

"Could we have maybe done that a little cleaner?" Timmons asked softly, with the 911 call on mute in his hands.

A sniff and then a face, Molly cursed. "Oops." She showed

the phone screen to Timmons, noting a text message with a sequence of four numbers tapped out but not yet sent. The title of the contact was DET 0037.

"Upside is we have his GPS track from his evening run. He started at a lake house in Mashpee, just up one of the two roads near Dino's. We should head there."

"Maybe after the ambulance arrives," Timmons touched Brian's shoulders. "Easy there, let it go. You tried."

Turning to Molly, Timmons checked her over. Weatherly had gotten off a shot, but she didn't appear hit. "Also, we're not even driving up that road without EOD and locals assisting." He pointed at the phone. "That could likely be a trigger code for some sort of self-destruct."

Molly gave a weak chuckle. "Someone should call Hobbs. He may want to be in the loop about this fast, before the locals get here."

Timmons said. "Simple self defense, he shot at you, you fired back."

Brian sat back on his heels. "Well, in her case, it may be a bit more complicated, as she has an active court date to address some issues from the last time she shot two people dead in this state."

"Oh, really?"

Molly sighed, dropped the mag out of her rifle, ejected the round and tossed the weapon on the sidewalk. "If they put me in cuffs again, I'm going to throw a fit."

Chapter 27

Lake House

"She did WHAT?" Hobbs cried, and then closed his eyes and intentionally banged his head against the headrest twice. Only after he got past the moment of frustration did he fumble for his notebook.

"Bad dude shot first," Jason answered from the front passenger seat of the hummer. "Oh, and your shirt is off by a button."

Hobbs had been halfway to changing out for a late evening run on base when Jason banged on his door and sent them back out. While there were some grumbles from the company, most of those were because the pizza and wings consumed suggested either a nap or workout was next after the long day. The older detective had simply yanked back on his pants over running shorts and followed Jason without question.

Until now.

"I've got to get this down carefully, Captain," Hobbs complained. "The paperwork alone on this whole engagement is going to be hell. Now that there's a homicide, it's just tripled in effort."

Jason held up a hand, cupped his ear, and spoke. "Yes, that'll be fine. We will wait off Nathaniel HWY, a big parking lot next to a pizza place. Can't miss it."

Hobbs frantically scratched down notes, then looked up to see Jason staring at him.

"Do you want to help? Call this number instead of scribbling and get them to send down a response team. We have a house one mile up the road, and we need to make absolutely sure it's safe before we investigate it. Make a call."

Putting down the pad of paper after scratching out one more note, Hobbs sighed and rang the number Jason had been given as the primary contact at Mass State Police if Charlie Company needed a high level intervention.

"They're sending down teams from Weymouth and over from Hyannis," Hobbs reported as he completed the call.

Jason struggled to get his chair assembled. From the height of the Humvee's seat, it wasn't easy. Both Hobbs and the driver moved to help, but he completed the unfolds, clicks and then butt smack on the pad on his own.

"ETA?"

"Hyannis should be here in maybe forty minutes, a few Mashpee units in five. The bomb squad from off cape? An hour and a change."

"What's your gut say? Remember, we have our own EOD guys with ODA 3430." Jason studied Hobbs. The careful detective, obviously sweating in the heat and not happy with the situation, was, however, demonstratively careful. Jason honestly desired his input. "Seriously. Who should go up that road? Our company? On the fringe of the law, technically; even with the Governor requesting us to take care of this? Or the locals.”

Hobbs, only a few years from retirement, had been employed continuously around the state since he graduated college and finished the police academy decades in the past. He knew the Weymouth team, and they were solid. But stories had been told of Cape Cod boys. There were a few books on the topic as well.

“Don’t let Hyannis clear the house, Jason. Delay them.” Hobbs frowned. “I know nothing specific; but I’d keep this a National Guard thing until Weymouth gets here.”

“I got a plan for that,” Jason chuckled, hearing sirens in the distance. “Can you keep the Masphee police here for me? I’ll be right back outside. And then we make sure Weymouth has the stick with us in support.”

Hobbs raised an eyebrow, but nodded, and Jason turned to wheel towards Dino’s.

Once inside, he smiled up at the hostess. Something about the dirty blond hair, green eyes and face full of freckles caused him to change his plan. “Ow, you are lovely, miss!”

Taken briefly aback, the woman colored. “Well, thank you... What can I do for you, mister?”

“You folks expect to get terribly busy tonight?”

She shrugged at the question. “Not really. No games on tonight. Likely to be a quiet Thursday.”

“Any chance I can chat with the manager for a bit? I likely have a bunch of people coming through, and may need to order some pies and wings for them, even though I already grabbed a tall stack earlier.”

The girl beamed. “Was that you guys? It’s not normal to have that many pizzas come through in the middle of the week."

"The house specials were killer," Jason answered her with a matching smile. "About that manager?"

"Oh, he's behind the bar," the woman said, and pointed towards the middle of the U-shaped building.

Jason put on his charm. "Thank you. Your name, miss?"

"Oh, I'm Lilly," the woman accepted his hand, and he shook it gently.

"Captain Jason Richardson." He gave a mini tug on the captured hand, almost as if teasing at kissing it.

"Nice to meet you, mister," Lilly lowered her hand and gestured towards the bar.

Following the hand and squeaking past the stools and the high surface, he locked his brakes. With a sigh, Jason pulled himself up to his feet and took one step to settle on a stool.

"What can I get for you?" the man behind the bar asked. He was in his late 50s, stout but not fat, lightly salted black hair and beard recently trimmed. He set down the glass he was cleaning and focused his full attention on Jason, noting instantly details on the full uniform and then the wheelchair behind the stool.

"Maybe a lower bar," Jason said, eyes scanning the pictures on the wall over the shelves of alcohol.

"Oh, we raise the bar here, not lower it, Army," the man said. His words were smooth as he settled both hands on the polished wood.

Jason drew one crayon from the pack of eight Brian had passed him for facilitating their joint pranking of Molly and set it on the bar as an answer to the man's challenge. Spinning the orange crayon, Jason gave it a little flick of his finger and the manager caught it before it fell into the sink.

"I have something potentially going on near here, and I have two requests. Any chance we can take over the tables on your left side?" Jason pointed to the long room opposite the pizza takeout desk and past the bar. "Consider it like a catering thing. I'll order food and drinks now to get them started. But I may need to keep some people occupied."

"And second?" the manager asked. He dropped two shot glasses on the counter and deposited the crayon in one of them.

"Do you know this man?" Jason asked. He took a chance, and flashed his cellphone to the man, with a picture of Weatherly on the screen.

"Ya," the manager said. "He's a regular. Normally just picks up pizzas, but occasionally sits for a while in the corner. Likes Allagash White."

"Anyone come here with him? Or associate with him? Or always alone."

"Hey, Lilly!" the manager called out, and the freckled hostess walked over quickly.

"Yup?"

"Who is the person who orders the Chorizo subs every Monday? Delivery most of the time. Usually your ticket. Lives just behind us?"

"Oh, that would be Mike."

"What's his address?" Jason asked, softly.

"Ah, 30 Quail Hollow Drive. He lives in the basement at the end."

"Hmmm," the manager said. He regarded Jason carefully.

"Hmm," Jason agreed with a nod.

"Hrrrm," the manager's voice shifted downwards into a growl.

A second crayon, this one yellow, clicked onto the bar. "I have to be careful to ration these out slowly."

"Just because you can barely stand on your own two legs doesn't mean I'm not willing to pick you up and throw you out of my place," the manager said.

"In about ten or fifteen minutes, a redhead girl is going to come through that door. You will know her when you see her. This Crayola is for her, and I would be honored if you would deliver it. Since she just capped one of the nation's most wanted terrorists just north of Johns Pond," Jason tapped his phone, which still had the picture up. "She gets a fucking crayon."

Jason continued, dropping his precious American Express. "This is for our tab. Put in another ten pizzas. Half pepperoni and half house. I need to use that room for a coordination location for the massive amount of law enforcement who are going to be arriving soon. Might as well get them fed."

Manager looked back and forth between the yellow crayon, the card, Jason's chair, and then the man's face. "I hadn't agreed to the use of space yet, captain."

"Good, since I need to add another request. May I borrow Lilly's apron and her car?"

"That guy was a terrorist?" The manger poured himself a shot of vodka in the second glass.

"Unfortunately, the worst kind. Home grown and well connected." Jason made a look to the room left. "I expect nothing to go down here. I just need to use the lure of food and space as a buffer to delay things happening elsewhere.

Got me?"

The manager shrugged and called back to Lilly. "Come here for a moment?"

She dutifully crossed over and rested against the bar, looking over at Jason. "What's up?"

"Your past due for your inspection sticker, right, girl?"

Lilly pulled back from the bar and flashed a glare over at Jason. "What is this?"

Jason held up both hands, palms out in a calming gesture. "What would it take to make your car pass?"

"This isn't making any sense," Lilly began backing away.

"Tires? Exhaust?" Jason asked gently.

Lilly shook her head and made a face. "Oh, just exhaust. You guys are being weird! And I thought you were cute."

Jason laid out ten one-hundred-dollar bills from a pouch in his vest. "These are yours, if I can borrow your car for a quick errand."

Lilly took the edge off her posture but didn't reach for her keys. "You just got a little cuter. If something happens to my car, is it covered?"

"I can promise you, Lilly," Jason said and stood from the stool on shaky legs. "You'll end up with a replacement."

"And the cash? In that case, drive it into the damn lake." The girl swiped the grand off the counter and replaced the pile with a fob.

Jason wheeled back outside, checked the ETA of the ODA 3430 crew from the base, and then looked up at the sun. He fired a text to Timmons, Brian, and Molly, who were all headed back to the empty lot next to Dino's. Message sent, he then spun over to find Lilly's Honda Element. In moments, he'd gotten himself, his chair, and the bag of takeout he'd stolen inside.

A brief spin through the parking lot where the rest of the company was holding brought him near PFC Hartwell. "Get in the back," he ordered, unlocking the doors of the surprisingly spacious SUV.

Key points; he thought to himself as he drove up the back road towards John's Pond. First, this car was known to Mike. A convoy of military vehicles was not. Second, the sun was down in minutes, and a runner this late in June coming back after dark was unlikely as it was very late. Third, trusted law enforcement EOD was a way out.

Hartwell asked from the back seat, as Jason's uniform top flew back in his face. "Sir? What are we doing?"

"The needful." Jason skidded the vehicle a bit, slowed down and got the bib from Dino's over his head without taking out a mailbox.

"One of our orders, Captain, was to ensure that neither you, Miss Turner nor Mister Deegan did something stupid. Are you in the process of doing something stupid?"

Jason laughed and looked up in the rearview, slowed to drive around a kid being pushed on his bike by his dad on training wheels, and slowed further to turn left on Quail Hollow.

"You are my backup and my witness. Think for a moment, Hartwell. If you were going out for a run. Would you be back by dark?"

The young man shrugged. "Usually?"

"Exactly... Usually. There is a second person at the residence. We don't know if he's involved or not; but his name is Mike. I'm going to get him away from his phone and out of the house. You backstop me. Got it?"

Hartwell sniffed and then shook his head. "This isn't cool, Captain Richardson."

Jason cautiously watched for kids and pets as he drove up the last gravel hill towards the top of the east ridge overlooking John's pond. Taking a left at a small twist where a private road broke right, he went the last few feet to pause behind a parked newer large pickup truck. The second vehicle in the driveway was a brand new Jeep Gladiator. One black cat gazed down at him from the second floor porch and rose to a sitting position.

"Stay low, but be ready to help me." Jason rolled down the windows, dropped his chair out, and then plopped his frame into it. Gathering the to-go order in his lap, he read the thermal paper receipt.

Jason struggled a little to go around the back of Lilly's car on the slope but got between the two trucks and approached the basement apartment door labeled "30 B". He knocked, rang the bell, and then rolled back a foot.

After a few moments, the door opened, and Jason held up the bag, recalling the items. "Dino's order! Cheeseburger with Cajun fries, and some garlic parmesan wings."

The man looked confused as he recognized the car, the bag, and the bib, but not the man.

He balked, but then took in the words as the smell evoked a hunger response. "I... That actually sounds good, but I ordered nothing tonight."

Jason feigned confusion and ripped the receipt off the bag with one hand while passing the burden over to the man with his right. "Hang on, let me check my phone."

"Isn't that Lilly's car?" the man said, pointing at the Honda.

Jason looked up. "Yeah, I'm trying to cover for her. I'm her boyfriend. They are on short staff tonight, and they got slammed."

The man apologetically pointed down at Jason's chair. "That's got to suck if you're doing their deliveries."

"Should have seen me try to deliver a pizza up a set of stairs last winter. I had to crawl up in a sled." Jason cursed, still looking down at his phone. "Well crap! So, it looks like you get this one on us. Can you check this number? I think they thought it was you?"

Jason held his phone out to the man, who took one more step out of the open door and looked down at the phone screen. Taking advantage of the movement, Jason gripped the man's hand with all of his strength, yanked, and spun the chair sideways. Completing the motion, Jason then smacked down one of the foot rests into Mike's chin.

While stunned, Mike had been in scraps before and responded quickly to the fact that he was suddenly in a fight. Jason noticed the man twist away and yank up his shirt to grab a pistol from inside his waistband. He dropped from the chair with both knees right on Mike's belly to block part two of that practiced draw.

While the blow to the stomach was lessened by an arm being across the area, the impact on soft tissues from a hundred and seventy-five pounds suddenly jamming something the size of a compact 9mm pistol into your appendix is like getting hit in the gut with a sledgehammer. Mike's body went into puke mode, and he lost the fight. Keeping that condition was helped by Jason rolling Mike to the side, first, and then second with a direct axe elbow to Mike's liver before shoving his face down into the asphalt.

His weight on Mike's back, Jason realized he'd forgotten anything relating to cuffs or zip ties.

"Hartwell?" Jason said. "Could use a little help here!"

A door closed on the car, and a shaky PFC Hartwell turned the corner, swore, and raised the barrel of his M4 to point at Jason's chest.

Chapter 28

Leverage

A spark of pain lit in Hartwell's eyes, and the young soldier threw down his cell phone and dropped his rifle. The second it fell, a voice cried out from down the hill. "FREEZE!"

Footsteps pounded around the back of the second vehicle and Brian came into view, struggling for breath, with his pistol pointed at Hartwell. The young man shook his head and pointed to Jason, tears in his eyes. "I couldn't take it! I'll help you, sir. I'm sorry. I couldn't take the deal!"

Brian and Jason locked eyes, but Brian instantly noted the dropped rifle and lowered his pistol.

"Secure that man, PFC!"

Wiping at tears, the young man complied and reached down to drag the still retching Mike out from under Jason. Flex cuffs came out of Hartwell's pack and tape applied to finalize the process.

Brian stepped closer to Jason, took two breaths, dropped to a knee, and groaned.

"What the hell?" Jason raised himself half up towards his chair, but with the long day and tough scuffle, he paused.

"Molly figured it out," Brian gasped, struggling for breath.

More foot falls and voices echoed in the distance. Then Jason heard a chainsaw far off.

Brian pointed to PFC Hartwell. "Weatherly wasn't detonating bombs, he was detonating people. Hartwell was 0037."

"They offered to pay for my grandma's hospice bill and my dad's mortgage if I killed you, sir."

"I got you, Hartwell!" Jason said strongly. "Search him. Get everything out of his pockets and away from his body. No keys, fobs, buttons, or bobs. Understood, son?"

"Yes, sir!" Heartwell said. He began tearing at clothes, still occasionally swiping at his eyes.

Timmons lead a group of four army soldiers around the corner and came up the hill, all huffing hard. The company sergeant took in the two men on the ground. As Mike was trussed and being systematically stripped and Hartwell performing the action, Timmons lowered his rifle for the last few steps. Two of the four behind Timmons immediately dove in to assist the PFC.

"Deegan, dude," Timmons said. "What the hell are you made of? A cheetah crossed with a rhino or some shit?"

Brian, still gasping for air, laughed and then almost retched. He tried to wave it off while accepting a bottle of water from Timmons.

"Let's get further away from this house while you explain," Jason patted Brian's arm and then hauled himself into his chair, with only a little help from Timmons.

They repaired to the bottom of the hill with one of the ODA sergeants, with Timmons backing Lilly's car down next to them. Settled on mostly level ground, Jason tossed his plate carrier back over his head from the back seat and pointed back towards HWY 151.

"What happened that way?"

"Road is blocked, Jason. A few minutes after you went on your little stupid ass crusade, the bridge went down. They're having to cut trees to make a ford to get the trucks up here."

Jason raised one eyebrow, then pointed between Hartwell, who still had a grim looking older sergeant standing very close to him, and Brian.

"And them?"

"Molly made a call out that the phone number Weatherly was sending a message to had been with our party. She narrowed it to Hartwell," Brian said, his eyes closed, back resting against the car tire.

"And when we heard that, we came looking for you," Timmons added. "Along with the EOD crew and gear Davis and I stole from the base. And then we found the bridge out. Then this gazelle, rhinoceros, beast man goes into cheat mode and tore off up the road."

"I think he's mad because you smoked him," Jason said to Brian, receiving a snort in reply.

The sound of trucks coming up the hill with most of the company, plus the EOD crew from the base, made Jason grin. Timmons received the nod from Jason to guide them up, and Jason relaxed back a bit into the chair. Then he reached down and grabbed Brian's shoulder. "You didn't have to do that."

"I almost shot that kid," Brian said. He then grabbed Jason's hand, hard. "And you didn't have to wheel your busted ass up here in some grand gesture of manliness."

Jason shook his hand free and then presented the string of secure texts from Mike's phone to Brian. The one highlighted showed Mike was about to initiate some sort of evil layer self destruct plan when the door rang.

"Okay.... Yeah... Never mind. Maybe you did," Brian frowned. "But why did he open the door?"

Jason tapped the car behind him. "Pretty young lady. I noticed the delivery driver's schedule. The hostess with the freckles and the cute backside is always their driver on Mondays. Mike always ordered delivery on Monday. He was just like us not too long ago. A blind mouse to the charm of a girl."

A bump and a sizzle of a flash bang rang out in the air, and then the power went out to the streetlights. Jason tensed at first and then sighed after hearing the smattering of "all clear" rang out in the comms channel and laid his head back.

"Are you okay, Brian?"

Brian groaned. "I'm gonna feel this in the morning. That was the most I think I've run in three months. You?"

Jason resettled himself in the chair.

"It's kind of weird," Jason said. "I hurt before I started. I hurt before I even woke up today; but something about getting a valuable piece of intel from the restaurant owner, and then driving this car up here, and using it to fake out and then take down a bad guy... Success dulls the pain."

"There's a quote I read, and have tried to incorporate into my life." Brian closed his eyes. "When all else fails, something must go. In the end, you are left with simply everything. You have everything you need, always. Everything is faith."

"Wow," Jason said. "That one, I'm going to have to take

some time to process. Also, hang on a second, I need to send a message."

Carl! Jason texted. *Pizza was good, but we have a potential Iron Horse issue.*

Jason waited for the reply dots to stop cycling.

Did someone in your company get contacted?

Shelving his frustration, Jason kept tapping. *Yes. Private First Class Augusta Hartwell.*

Noted.

Did you catch it? Jason carefully planned his text, as he knew anything which reached Carl was being watched by more than him, Carl, Brian, and any random squirrels in the trees above them.

Yes.

With a sigh of relief, Jason asked one more question. *How many in total were tagged and approached?*

... I shouldn't share that. ... 18.

Locking his phone and putting it in his pocket, Jason banged his head against the car.

"What?" Brian pulled himself up to a sitting position. "Something happened?"

"Eh," Jason waved a hand. "This doesn't leave this little corner of the Hollow, but what's your best guess about how many of our off-the-cuff, last minute marginally legal company were directly contacted by outside actors since we left Georgia for this hunt? Like that poor kid over there."

Brian shrugged and pointed to the Hummer a hundred feet away, which now had Mike in the back. A very determined PFC Hartwell was focused on filling out a form on a clipboard to complete the "arrest" under the National Guard rules.

"Less than 90 people knew of what we were doing, or were directly involved. Okay, make that around 100 if you include the crew of the C-130. Despite that," Jason sipped some water. "A total of 18 were not just directly identified, but contacted. Each via the software algorithms just like what we recovered from 4510 Iron Horse in Kentucky. The same code and hardware we all almost died for three months ago."

Brian winced. "That's a lot. That's bad, man. Really bad."

Jason pointed his thumb to the west behind him. "Upside is. That nuke lab and everything to keep it running is at the bottom of the water. Olivia got a bunch of intel and scuttled the lab. That parts over."

"Heard," Brian nodded. "Also, I'll miss the other Brian. He was a good dude. Guy gave me a bunch of pointers, and sent me to some YouTube videos to help Molly's shoulder. Sorry Honeysuckle got hit."

"Ya, same. I'll likely offer to go to his house after we get home, since I'll be the closest. I hate making death calls."

"Hey," Brian shrugged. "At least you didn't shoot anyone tonight. For me, that's almost worse. Almost."

Looking up at the moon beginning to shine over the lake to the north, Jason nodded.

"Sure. Night's still very young. Speaking of, how's Molly? Since she did off a human, did she take it well?"

"Ya, she was more worried that she'd have to be taken to jail again," Brian said.

They both winced as a sharp thump was both felt and heard from up the hill.

"Eh, that one was in the bomb truck," Jason waved. "Davis likely found something his boys didn't like and made it vaporware."

"Got it." Brian massaged an ear. "I think Molly is good. The only issue long term maybe her second guessing firing sooner, since the guy got a shot off. Though, pistol at 70 yards vs rifle?"

"Particularly in her hands," Jason chuckled. "Ya, nope; not taking those odds any day. Just wanted to make sure her head was right."

Brian laughed. "That's sort of what this whole side mission has been for the three of us. A test to make sure our heads were right."

"I can see that," Jason said. He gave the captain's patch on his chest a pat and thought back to how Josiah baited and then played him up into this gig. It was a test on several levels.

"One more thing..." Brian asked a bit more softly, looking out over the lake as the moon beams began painting the surface. "Are you okay with the chance of there being an us? A thing between Molly and I?"

"Brian, if you ask that girl to marry you, I'll get my sad ass out of this chair, put on a dress and offer to be her bridesmaid if it's what you two need. I will probably cry."

Jason heard a click and went cold. "Brian... did you just...."

The sound of a marginally repressed chuckle was book ended by the click of a text message being sent in the night before another thump up the hill.

"Don't worry," Brian mused, "I just sent that picture to

Collin for safe keeping. Also, I've worn dresses before; it's not bad. Lots of air flow."

A tremendous splash sounded across the pond, and then a second thump and then a loud bang rocked the trees.

"Forgot to mention to you," Jason said. "When I found out the bar owner was a former USMC, I passed him a token for Molly for when she gets there."

"Really?" Brian asked between taking pictures of their view of the lake. "How'd that go?"

"I'm pretty sure he had his hands on a Colt .45 under the counter for most of the conversation. But he accepted the assignment. A yellow Crayola is sitting in a shot glass ready for our Molly."

Brian snickered his approval.

Jason laughed. "I think I feel sorry for Detective Hobbs. He's tried hard to work with us. But we just planted him as the primary liaison between something like seven government agencies who are all pretty much as we speak arriving at the bar."

"Hmm," Brian shrugged. "Hobbs did cuff Molly to a bed for hours. Still, I agree. He's not a bad guy."

"Which is why I threw him a little party. What better way to keep people listening than give them a bunch of food? I never realized how useful something like a stout credit card was before Las Vegas."

Jason looked back and forth up the road, locked his eyes on a bush a few feet away from the car, and struggled to get to his feet. "I gotta piss."

Brian first turned away, and then shrugged, stood and set a steadying hand on Jason's shoulder, and unzipped himself.

"This is fucking awkward," Brian said.

"If you cross the streams, I'm going to punch you."

Mission accomplished, Jason leaned heavily against the car, but kept his legs. "Huh, my damn left calf didn't cramp up this time."

Jason clenched his fists. "We have to deal with this hotspot finding crap next. That almost a third of Charlie Company with us here has been specifically targeted, like PFC Hartwell, with careful application of leverage. I'm just glad the kid didn't off me, but now he has to deal with the stress of knowing he could have, and that he considered it."

"I'm really glad I didn't have to shoot him," Brian subconsciously drew and re-holstered his pistol after checking the chamber. "I have an idea, though. Not super into the tech crap, but I understand the basic premise. So seventy of us were active on our devices; phones, smartwatches, laptops, and mostly clumped or moving together for a few days. That's what this software detected, right? The clumping?"

"Essentially," Jason said. He reached into the car and drew a bottle of water from his pack, then crashed into his chair. "The hardware at 4510 showed us how they built this technology, but it was like our BattleBoxes. That server kit was generation 1. Our gen 1 kit was a mish-mosh of hardware we cobbled together and installed in our own cars and stations to figure out how to solve the problem. Then we iterated and are on gen 4 now that we have a solution framework. So are they; iterating."

Brian tapped his chin. "What if we just... Added something like... everywhere? Ah! Molly said she was doing this random trick while we were in Baku. She was downloading YouTube videos in the background to hide her footprint. Kind of like how a sniper may scare random game to hide his moves. Redirect the noise."

"Hmmm." Jason took a long look over the lake through the clearing and nodded. "If we built up enough point sources, and scatted them ideally in IP space, that might have legs. If a radio over here in Mass, for example, also appeared to be squawking in Arizona, and Oregon, and Austin, that signal could just be enough to confuse the code. I'll have to think about it hard and run some thoughts past Molly. We can fake hardware IDs, but aren't currently doing it actively in duplication."

"I saw the look on that kid's face, Jason. We must stop that from being possible. We can't let good kids like Hartwell get burnt."

"I hear you," Jason smirked at his use of the phrase. "I am hearing you."

Chapter 29

After party

"Oh, forgot to mention it to you," MD sipped a Guinness. "Molly shot Weatherly."

Olivia shrugged. "He dead?"

MD snorted and almost dropped the bottle. "Yeah; he dead."

"Good girl," Olivia turned and looked out over the pool. Petty Officer Smith, in a fetching one-piece, was having a blast playing essentially grab-ass with a pair of the Seals from Team X and one of the RDI kids from New Mexico. Damion and Cynthia were chatting near the massage jets in the shallow end, maintaining an appropriate distance, sort of.

As Olivia had just sent out the call over their chat app of a blanket invite, with catered food arriving in the next half an hour, more of their party would show up at any moment from the boy's house down the beach.

"They get anything good from Weatherly's house?" Olivia turned and included Sam in that question.

Still in her full uniform after just returning from a briefing at Kadena Field with the new base commander, she wiped sweat from her brow and winced. "Yes and, well, big yes. I'm being sent back to take over the investigation. Some people in CID didn't like the fact that we were out of the loop on the whole hunt and then kill thing Charlie Company was given on US soil. Normally, that would have been us running the investigation alongside the FBI."

"You people and not some," MD quoted in the air. "Trumped up corporal with a god complex. Or so I was recently lectured."

"Oh, here's Nori!" Olivia announced, seeing him and Al unlatch the gate to the pool.

Sam rolled her eyes and then noticed a shadow hanging behind her. Hong Nori Lin picked her up by her armpits and slung her out into the middle of the deep end of the pool like she was a sack of rice. Without looking back over his shoulder, he picked back up his bag and towel, reacquired the apple he was eating and went into the house to change into shorts.

"Oh, he dead too," Trevor laughed, snapping a picture of his daughter stripping off her uniform topper as she struggled to the edge of the pool, furious anger radiating from her.

"I tried to warn her!" Olivia complained, unable to keep the smile from her face as the dripping wet Samantha Sanders stalked over to the table. Cell phone, keys and knife slapped down on the wood, uniform top smacked to the ground, and then she took off running in her wet boots.

"Are you okay with that?" MD checked with Trevor.

The older man shrugged. "Bout damn time someone kicked her ass other than her mom; the Lord knows I've tried."

"Eh, you did all right," Olivia raised her glass of unsweet

tea. "To trying."

"I'll take that." MD tapped the rim with his beer, and Trevor added his goombay smash. "Cheers."

Something about MD's inflection made Olivia narrow her eyes at him. Leaning back, arms crossed and glower set to level three, she waited for him to spill whatever it was which crossed his queue.

MD calmly set one of his phones on the table in front of her, screen unlocked, and a fingerprint programming request prompt up.

"You are now the acting director; RDI Special Project Operations, Olivia Kuznetsov. Lady Olivia, I surrender to thee, my bat phone. May thy blood run hot, and head run cool. My will be done. The pointy hat is now yours."

Not expecting that, she dropped her jaw and looked over at Trevor, then back at MD, realizing that he was serious, despite the silly oath.

"You aren't joking," Olivia pointed at Trevor. "First, you can't step down. Second, if you did, it would be him that should take your place. I've barely been with RDI for four months!"

"He knew better than to even ask me," Trevor sighed. "I'm where I need to be. Besides, us regional managers are the ones who get to PICK the directors."

"Did you just wink at me?"

"Olivia..." MD pointed at the phone. "I said acting... You have like six months to mess it up, if you don't want the position full time. Secure that phone, woman!"

Uncrossing her arms with a huff, Olivia locked the phone to her thumb, reset the pin and then changed the avatar from the simple AI generated shield and sword MD had been using to a proper purple bunny rabbit wielding a spear. Setting the phone down on the table with finality, she clicked her teeth. "There! Happy now?"

"You could always throw him in the pool," Trevor suggested, making an "up up" gesture with his hands.

"Hmm," Olivia considered for a moment, replaced her glower with a menacing grin, and rose to her feet in a flash.

"OH, SHIT!" MD tried to dive sideways out of his chair, but the strong woman caught him mid sprawl, lifted him into the air, walked to the pool edge and then sent him flying.

While she admired her work for a moment, hands on hips, Olivia realized she was in trouble. Fred and Ivan had walked up behind her while she basked in her triumph. Fred scooped her legs, while Ivan captured her arms. The two men swung her back and prepared.

"One... Two... THREE!" They yelled together, gathering momentum.

Olivia screamed as she was launched halfway across the pool at the apex of the third swing.

Chapter 30

Next Steps

"So, what now?"

Brian looked over at Molly, resting against the wall in a hallway outside of one of the large gyms in the rehab facility in Columbus, where they had all spent too much time.

He took in carefully the details. How she had put up her red hair into a loose ponytail, rather than the brutally taught one she always seemed to favor when she was in pain. How her nails had been trimmed carefully, instead of with haste. That she had remembered to put on her watch, a gift from her brother on the day he left for basic training while she was a teenager. Those little things mattered. The cute redhead next to him was calm, neat, and composed. She had gotten back to her ground, but was now dangerously close to questioning the methods of that journey.

"You're not a killer," Brian knew what she was thinking, but he wasn't sure if she was aware of the pending internal struggle. "I can see where your head is at, Molly. Just because you can kill doesn't mean you are a killer."

"I guess I could choose to view it that way," Molly paused

and smiled a bit as Jason completed a circuit of out and back walking on the bars and accepted a high-five from his rather attractive trainer. "That was hard! Damn."

"Didn't your brother call you last week? Have you called him back?"

Molly looked away. "Eh, actually, want to drive down? My niece's birthday is on July 4th. While he was just asking if I was okay, I sort of didn't answer the question about the invite since I was too afraid to figure out how to make a trip in their direction."

"I'd be game for that."

"I really want to get what little garden we can in first," Molly nodded. "But since you are game, I was thinking of renting a car for the trip. Going a few days early. Maybe camping in the keys?"

"Saying my old Camry can't make it?"

"Brian," Molly made a sour face at him. "It doesn't have AC, and it's the middle of the summer. I kind of like the car, but it's like an eighteen hour drive from here to my brother's."

"I finally got the insurance check back from my shot up truck," Brian added. "Might as well replace it now. What better way to break in a new ride than a road trip?"

"What would you get?" Molly asked, and Brian picked up on the look in her eyes. She had quite a bit more passion for driving than Brian would ever manage, and almost as much natural skill behind the wheel as Collin.

"I was thinking about a minivan."

Molly's eyes bulged, and she inhaled sharply at the horror. "Oh, please! No?! We can just take your Camry."

"Well, what would you pick? If you had your choice?"

Molly thought hard at the question. The first thing which came to mind was the white Toyota HiLux with 4WD, manual transmission and lockers which she had driven hard in Baku. She had chased down a nuclear weapon on its attack run in that truck. Then used said truck to disable the launcher system by yanking the mechanism until it fell sideways. And while full of holes and abused in all kinds of ways, the truck still got the warhead away to safety and MD to the hospital with her behind the wheel. It never let her down. The picture that Trevor sent her of that white truck sitting on a wrecker rollback on its way to being vanished was one of her favorite keepsakes from the Baku adventure.

While that image of a stout truck was in her head, she realized this was a turning point in their relationship. "I picked the tractor, Brian. You pick a vehicle."

"I think you'd look fine in a minivan," Brian baited.

Rolling her eyes, Molly added to the deal. "NOT a minivan. Anything else."

Brian nodded. "You know, you also look damn fine in a uniform too, miss Molly."

Snorting, she shook her head, blushed, and looked down at the floor for a moment to compose her next salvo. "Not as good as you in those shorts last night."

"It was all I could find!" Brian groaned, also colored and growled, not happy about how soft about the middle he had become.

In a show of solidarity, the party over in Okinawa had been live streamed to them at a hotel outside of Fort Bragg where they had stayed the night before. Catching a ride back to Fort Benning at 0600 had been tough, given the few extra drinks they had consumed with their new and old friends in Charlie company. They still made it to Columbus in time for Jason to catch one of his well-needed PT appointments on the way to dropping him home and picking up Brian's car.

"I'm open for more, if you are, Brian," Molly set her hand on his arm, meeting his eyes.

"The fact that I get street credit for taking you home with me is enough," Brian held back the other words he almost said.

"Oh, is that what I am? Street credit?" Molly challenged, unable to keep the grin from twisting up one corner of her mouth.

"Of course." Brian turned, touched her other arm, and leaned down. Just before touching her lips, a squeak of tires braking suddenly on the floor behind them echoed against the walls.

"Really, kids?" Jason admonished. "Get a room!"

Before Brian could break away, Molly grabbed his neck, arched up and kissed him.

"Or... not? I guess?" Jason turned away, and headed off towards the exit door. "Yesh!"

Molly broke the kiss, tried to breathe for a moment, released her death grip on his neck and then grabbed her pack. The drop for the laptop bag allowed Brian to have moved a few feet further towards the door. As she was catching up, he completed the joke while pointing ahead to Jason. "See, street credit."

With a hiss through her teeth, Molly wound up and slapped the large man in the ass as hard as she could with her good hand.

At the blow, which stung, Brian grunted and bent over. At first, he choked on his laughter because of the absolute shock of the precise blow. Molly grabbed him to make sure he was okay, suddenly worried that she had hurt him, but when the laughter rolled forth from the man, she giggled alongside her friend.

Jason turned halfway through the door at the echo of the spank. He watched his friends for a few moments in their awkward embrace of sorts.

"I am alive," Jason smiled, and felt tears well in his eyes. "Oh, I am. Alive."

Chapter 31

Future Work

"We can't let this software stay alive," Charlotte Marlow, spoke with authority before the committee in her role as Program Manager. "The NSA concludes we must apply ourselves to both remove active infestations of this software in our infrastructure, while also adding tools to the community to lessen the potential impact of the software across our armed services, contractors, and resources."

"You are heard, Marlow," Berger, now head of the committee by seniority, nodded his head and sipped his coffee. "That conclusion will be taken under advisement. I expect us to act to cut contracts for investigating the scope of the Iron Horse 4510 software's impact, and also actively attempting to intercept and terminate the actions of the software."

"While also," Marlow looked down, and read a note from Jason Richardson in her texts. "Mitigating future potential for this or similar packages to cause harm to our operations?"

"Of course, Mrs. Marlow."

"As my first step on this committee," MD pulled himself off mute. "I would like to move to create a contract request for bid to mitigate the chance of this software to identify, isolate, and then target our resources. I have in my hands an example of a proof of concept from Jason Richardson at RDI."

"So entered the agenda for the next meeting, MD," Berger sketched down a note. "Next up, we are reviewing a request to extend a contract with HawkWorks for contract HW-783-29316. The DOD has fronted an additional 10.6 million dollars over the baseline to field a prototype. All parties please submit your votes before the next meeting for confirmation. Necessary summary docs are in your inbox for review."

"I have to drop the call now," MD waved and was given a clear thumbs up from Berger. "I've got another one I can't miss."

MD sipped coffee from an exceptional little instant espresso machine he'd acquired from the bosun of the now sunk *Crystal Dream* in exchange for a pack of smokes and a six-pack of the darkest beer he could bribe the kid who delivered supplies to the docks to source.

"Go ahead, Jason," he opened the second meeting, and nodded for Olivia to join him from her perch across the second floor library they had adopted as their mutual inside office at the house in Okinawa. "Sorry, we couldn't do this in person, but we had been still stuck in Guam for a week."

"Yah, what was up with that?" Jason smiled and waved to Olivia as she pulled up a chair in the camera feed.

"Stupid political bullshit mashed up with international immigration law."

"I warned you, Olivia," MD shook his head. "See, Jason; we left Okinawa by smuggling ourselves out while the ship was taking on fuel. It was a cheap trick, but the sly move kept us off radar. When we got in port in Guam, offloading the crew from the *Dream* was all legitimate. They left one port and arrived at another. Sure, some of them were dead, but the flow of taxable bodies and goods was maintained. And since we left Okinawa without an exit stamp... We were in limbo."

"They finally gave up and shipped us back to Okinawa a few days ago," Olivia smirked. "All my good bathing suits were here. All I packed was the stupid one-piece for the mission."

MD checked his watch. "I've got to make this fast. You got something, Jason?"

"Ya," Jason shuffled a note pad around and opened up a share with a picture. "Josiah says hi, Olivia."

The woman raised an eyebrow at a funny picture of Josiah taking a selfie with hot sauce dribbling down his face, midway through consuming a hot wing.

"He finished up his... am I allowed to say interrogation? Let's go with a grooming session with the dude we found at James Weatherly's house. A guy named Mike Adams."

"You mean the guy whose face you bashed in with your wheelchair?" MD asked.

"I was mad, and he had a gun," Jason snorted. "And also, there were a few thousand pounds of C4 in the house. Moving on."

Jason clicked ahead a picture and Olivia recoiled from the laptop screen, hands raised and eyes closed.

"Gah!"

"Is that..." MD leaned forward. "Interesting technique."

The offending picture showed a pair of swollen feet with hundreds of sewing needles jabbed in at all kinds of angles and depths.

"Yes, apparently torturing me with things I can't eat wasn't enough for Josiah yesterday. So, good and bad bits. Good is that this Mike critter could provide some intel. Bad in that he had been mostly stepping back from the more active stuff and was downgraded to playing the World of WarCraft and watching over Weatherly's cats while he was away. Dude had a bit of a meltdown and got taken off the A-team of doom."

"Please tell me the good includes that picture being off the damn screen," Olivia complained.

"She has a thing about feet," MD explained, and received a slap on the arm.

Jason stopped the share. "First, the house in Mashpee. The method of how it was selected for a safe house and purchased is known for this and others. Just like how RDI blows its spare budget at the end of any year, snagging up foreclosures which look interesting, Weatherly's group has been doing the same. Mike could confirm that the entire organization, outside of elements like the direct action groups and implanted folk, all are randomly dispersed at foreclosed or in transition properties. A few factors seem present; access to high-speed internet, coastal locations, and tourist destinations with easy access to multiple airports or port facilities."

"Sounds like they took a page from RDI's own playbook like you said," MD shook his head. "That's pretty much our menu list for the safe-houses we have been establishing for contract work globally."

"Hey," Olivia opened her eyes, verified the screen was clear and relaxed. "And that menu got us those outstanding Air-BnBs in Okinawa. Best tan of my life. Which I squandered, being quarantined on a greasy ship for a week."

"There was an incident with her sunbathing on the ship's bow," MD received another slap to his arm. "Okay, was there anything else other than the methods and dispersion configuration we could get?"

"You mean from the 1047th needle?" Jason spoke blandly, watching Olivia for a reaction. He got one as she cringed and leaned back. "Actually yes. And hella-yes. Mike had been to two of such prepared safe locations, one recently. The older one is in Key West, but the last was just a couple of months ago in Ft. Lauderdale. Also, he saw Sydney Brenner there. Wasn't the first time he had contact with the lab lead engineer."

"How can we trust that?"

"He'd been scratched by the man's cat. Spicy critter, from what I've heard."

"That cat is in Olivia's room right now," MD laughed. "And ya, the dude has opinions."

"Expert opinions, I hope?" Jason winked, and MD nodded.

Olivia held her fourth slap. "Before I react to that. And I will take care of that and the reminder of how it was acquired," Olivia shuddered, recalling the image once more. "I'm sensing a tone here from you. Aren't you back in Columbus?"

"As of today, but about to not be," Jason carefully made sure the camera couldn't see Melissa Long in the kitchen doing her makeup at the table and opened the video. "Heading back to Bragg. It seems Major Dickson really didn't want to come back to command Charlie Company until his leave expired, and since I sort of had the slot, we extended the Title 32 until he returns. And I believe we are going to receive orders today to go checkout a few real estate locations in North Carolina which may be in enemy hands."

"And you agreeing to this, did it have something to do with a newly promoted blonde army E-5?"

Jason shrugged, but kept his poker face to the max. "I do not know of whom you speak. And I do have to hit the road."

"Be safe, kid," MD said warmly. "Still cards in hands out there. We all need to keep our eyes up."

"Same, Jason," Olivia laughed. "And tell Melissa I need to meet her."

"You two are scary when you're both on the same screen, you know that? See you soon." Jason laughed and waved before cutting the connection.

After packing up his laptop, Jason turned the lights off for the last time in his short-term apartment in Columbus and breathed a sigh of relief. While he stepped out of the doorway and closed and locked it while standing, he had to almost immediately drop back down into his ready chair in the interior hallway.

Melissa Long picked up his last bag from the floor and dropped it in his lap. Jason grunted at the weight, but wheeled ahead just fast enough to pinch her in the rear.

"Hey!"

It was now time to face the fire of the summer day.

Afterward

If you have made it this far in the Fallen Apples series, I feel it is necessary to offer some words of thanks. This story means a great deal to me. It is a tribute to fallen friends, and an escape to allow my mind and soul to sample from the path not taken. Seriously; thank you for offering your time to read my work. It is an honor to be selected to share with you.

I never served in the military, though I *did* come very close to signing on with the United States Navy at seventeen years old. As I would have needed a parental signature, and this was in the years before the tragic events in 2001, that wasn't likely to have happened. Also, since my dad was a cryptography specialist and radio technician in the Air Force... Ya, that really would not happen.

And now I'm distracting myself from what's important. This book is a few days late.

I'll be honest here. I woke extra early on Independence Day, before the Maine dawn, and sat down to take one last stab at clearing off the to-do list for getting this book out the door. Then another project came on my screen and claimed my morning dose of effort as I sorted out cat food and coffee operations. When my time ran out, I grabbed my old beat up tuba and went to the state capital to march in a parade with a town band to celebrate the holiday.

(Okay, fine; I didn't actually march!) Most of the band is on the older side, and we have a float a solid 27 piece ensemble. My wife took our son, who did actually march, to a small town parade for the last time with our cub scout pack, as he will move on to the local boy scout troop in the Fall.

Then I went home for lunch, fixed the tractor, broke a chain saw, and spent the mid-day listening to this book and clearing land. As the day wound down, tractor-ops turned to shower and a drive with my family — and my venerable horn — for an evening concert. Our town band concluded the performance with a segue into the fireworks at Booth Bay with the last bars of the National Emblem March.

So, when I put something other than July 4th as the official publication date on this novel; please forgive me. I had to honor the day. And I had to reflect here on that meaning to seal this book.

On the following pages, you will find my first teaser! Book five: *From the Ashes*, has been ready for quite some time on the inside. It will go to the spa next week, and soon after will receive a cover to match its brothers and sisters on the shelf. I expect to be ready to punt it out the door into the wild before September. While *Ashes* will be the last of the *Fallen Apples* story, it is not the end of the line for the characters and the universe.

Before I explain where this story is going, I should mention a few bits about where this has been. To do that, we have to show where it started. The core concept ties directly into my excuses for being tardy.

Have you ever needed to do one thing, been required to do something else, and then simply gave up on your entire set of wants as you know to the tips of your toes it was impossible to do all three? Life frequently provides us with such a confusing menu of options. But unlike the trope "fast, strong, cheap; pick any two," in actions and decisions on the daily, we often are forced to select only one option.

The first words which flowed from keys written in this universe were:

"All I want right now is to sit down with a
good book and a great cup of coffee," said MD.

As that was written at least three virtual machines and a handful of laptops in my rear-view mirror, the year might be off, but I recall that those words were tapped out on a Christmas morning at around 0600. It was snowing outside, and I had a cat on my lap. The year was most likely 2017. On that morning, I wanted nothing more than to stay in that warm chair, watch the flakes fall in the edges of my vision, and write out the dream I had experienced. You find that solution set channeled directly into my characters.

Now, eight (ish?) years later, here we are. I fought tooth and nail to draw this story out of the depths of my mind. The implementation details changed course with time, necessity, and discovery. The core remained the same. I wanted the characters to struggle with the truth of the human condition. The battle within.

Many more things are coming for these characters after the series' finale. In the fall of 2025, a completed follow on with Jason Richardson at the helm of a militia company launches into the futuristic dystopia science-fiction realm exploring a civil war titled: *Iron Brigade: Battle for Maine.* Present-day actions will continue with the current team as they track down a pharmaceutical black market manufacturing network in Mexico and a human trafficking ring in central Europe, with an expected release date in Spring of 2026.

For now, I leave you with a note of hopeful optimism. As much as the crisp Maine morning air is calling me outside to go cut wood, I'll stay at my keyboard and get these words into your hands!

Please turn the page to receive a glance into the last *Fallen Apples* novel.

Sample Chapter 1: Road Trip (From the Ashes)

Molly Turner signaled to exit I-95 and reached behind to the back seat to tap Brian Deegan's chest. Their destination was a KOA campground just on the edge of the Florida Everglades and she needed to pee. Also, the hungry truck needed expensive diesel, and her hand hurt from driving for the last four hours.

"Wake up," Molly gently repeated, a tap on a large elbow within range. "Pulling off. This is our exit."

Deftly maneuvering the truck and trailer combination to take the off-ramp in light morning traffic, Molly verified her direction for the nearest diesel via the helpful signs on the ramp, signaled for a right, and settled the rig behind a small delivery truck at the stoplight. As she pulled out from the light, a silver minivan cut around her fast and sped ahead to get caught at the next red light. Easing into a break in the traffic, a groan issued from the back seat. Brian Deegan grunted, accidentally let out a fart, and sat up.

"Sorry," he apologized, cracking open a Moxie soda from the cooler in the back and taking a long swig.

Molly snorted a laugh, made a face in the rear-view mirror, and rolled down the front windows. At the green light, Molly noticed the same silver minivan signaled a lane change and cut into the car section of a large gas station to their left. Something about the van bugged her. Seeing it leave the interstate here bugged her more. She wasn't sure, but it looked close to the make and model to the one which had been hovering in her blind spot an hour north near Cape Canaveral.

"I'll text my brother when we get to the gas station," Molly checked Brian in the rearview. "Assuming I remember. Remind me if I don't?"

"Text Brother John," Brian nodded. "Aye. Do we need to bring anything when we drive down in the morning?"

"He said nothing needed, but I'll still bring a drink offering. What wine goes with fish? White, right?"

"Depends on the fish." Brian yawned and shook his head to get the sleep to let him go. "They're out fishing all day. What did John say they were going for?"

Molly made a face and checked her texts. "The day at sea is why we're staying the night up here. He had back-to-back charters today. Ah, morning was tarpon, and night cruise for tuna and Mahi."

"Could go either way then," Brian nodded. "Chardonnay can't go wrong. I'll make up a quinoa side salad and maybe something with zucchini, if we can find some fresh veggies."

"John said we didn't need to bring anything, Brian. I figured we could get away with a bottle of wine."

Brian shook his head. "If you think for a moment, I'm showing up at a Marine's house without some sort of culinary offering. Ain't gonna happen, little miss. I'm hoping he has a good grill for the steaks I've got marinading in the fridge. The grill that came with the camper sucks at searing."

Molly groaned a little and signaled to turn into the larger gas station on the right. Brian overdid the food thing at times, though his track record for positive experiences in that line of culinary expanse granted him a pass. Pulling the truck into the line at the large diesel pumps, she reflected on how the 2-year-old Chevy 2500 HD was behaving, just as her dad had taught her to do while on road trips. A simple little vibration ignored could turn into a breakdown if gone unchecked. That same careful mentality had allowed her to limp along an old Subaru for five years in the salty New England environment. Nothing really tweaked her about this truck, so she marked the relative levels of fuel and diesel exhaust fluid in her mind and settled into park.

The new-to-them truck had towed the 32 ft camper down from where it had been stashed for almost four months at a farm in Kentucky without issues. While the truck was technically Brian's, the camper was a "loaner" from a coworker at Refit and Design International (RDI) and belonged to Justin Tarbert. As that particular RDI contractor had been off the continent for much of the last year between contracts, the camper had gotten used for a few adventures.

Brian watched carefully as Molly lined up the rig behind an Estes freight truck and nodded as she gave plenty of space to bring things square. "I should run in. Are you good to find a spot to park after the fill up, Molly? Try to not have to back into it. It's difficult."

"I'm good, Brian," she looked over and patted his hand that had gripped the seat. "Go."

With a nod, Brian hopped out into the steamy Florida air and went inside to find the bathroom. Though she had to go herself, the large man's recent injuries had given his 30-year body the gift of inconsistent lower feedback. Taking a rifle round to a kidney does that to a person.

Moving the vehicle up as the tractor trailer pulled away, Molly stopped in the right spot to access the fill nozzles. It took her a moment to find the wallet in her bag. Pausing only to adjust the small Glock 43x in its holster on her left-hand side, she made sure her shirt was covering it, and went for the pumps.

As she fumbled with the leather fold to extract her card, a Florida DOT officer walked over while wiping his hands with a rag.

"Morning, miss," the officer checked the truck tag and then wrote it down on his clipboard. He was about to say something else when her fumbling launched the wallet from her hand and almost land it in the diesel drip spot near the pump. "You okay there?"

Holding up her right hand, which was now on its third cast following two surgeries, she nodded. "Mostly. Just I'm right handed. Sometimes I forget this one doesn't want to close all the way."

Nodding at the explanation, he observed as she reacquired her wallet and card, swipe into the machine, and insert both the fuel and DEF nozzles into their required ports.

"Hrm..." the officer checked the placard on the side of the trailer. "How much does this trailer weigh in at?"

"I think around 8900," Molly had been lightly briefed by Brian about why it's important to be careful with vehicle weights while towing, but she would rather he was here to answer this officer's questions. After the long drive, she struggled to remember the terms he used. "We scaled before leaving Kentucky a few days ago. I can probably find the receipt from the truck stop."

"Hrm..." the officer repeated. "Do you have a commercial license?"

"I..." Molly stuttered, noted the DEF completed, and moved to return the nozzle. Since she tried to grab it with her marginally functional right first, and was being questioned, AND had to pee, she, of course, almost dropped it.

"Might I ask? What happened to that hand of yours?"

With a sigh, Molly quickly played back the events in her head. Then she filtered those events with what she could share. Since the event which injured her hand, not to mention several other parts of her now 25-year-old body, had gone viral on YouTube, Molly had some freedom to speak. "I took a few rounds to the hand and forearm, officer. Really shouldn't talk much about it."

"Hrm!"

The officer really seemed to like that expression. He waved at his face a few times to send away one of the bees, which had been buzzing around the trash bucket next to the pumps.

"I'm gonna ask you for your license, registration, and proof of insurance. You have a temporary Georgia tag, but the trailer is tagged in Maine, not Georgia. Why is that?"

Molly remembered Brian mentioning something about Maine trailer registrations being super cheap, so everyone used to register there until the other states caught on and locked it down. "Owner's from Maine, officer. We're just borrowing it so I can visit my brother's family down here. Haven't seen them in over a year."

"Is that so?"

The officer, Hamilton, according to his name tag Molly noted as he had gotten close enough for her to read it, accepted her license.

"One moment, I'll have to raid the glove box." Molly paused as she planned for how she needed to step up into the truck and then realized her shirt would ride up, and second, that there was a pack of spare magazines for her Glock in the door pocket. He would likely see one or the other; or both. Not to mention the plate carriers and long arms in the back seat under a blanket. The reminder from Brian echoed back in her mind. She kept her hands far from her body and still. "I believe I'm required to inform you I am licensed to carry a firearm in all states, and am doing so at this time."

"Hrm." Molly was tiring of that non-committal response. It seemed to convey some meaning, but was difficult for her to decipher. "All states. Federal? What agency?"

"The letter is a blanket to my employer, issued through the Secret Service," Molly nodded to the truck. "I have a copy in my bag if you need it. It's in the back seat."

"Why didn't you show me your badge, then?"

Molly shook her head. "I don't have one. I'm a contractor."

"For the Secret Service?"

"Not currently, officer, ah, Hamilton," Molly tried to play the pity card again. "Last gig was for the Department of Defense. As I mentioned; security contracts. We're just both down here visiting family."

Frowning, he carefully examined Molly from her hiking boots to her red hair, rather messy from the day and night of travel. Her small athletic form topped out at five and a half feet. Hamilton shrugged. "Tell you what. You don't show me yours, and I won't show you mine. That work for you?"

"Of course." Molly did her best to smile. It was an honest expression, backed up by the truth that Molly really didn't want to add getting in a scuffle with law enforcement to her growing historical record.

At the wave from Hamilton, Molly climbed up into the truck and pulled the pack of documents out of the glove box. Back outside with the folder, she extracted the registrations for truck and trailer. Insurance forms for both were paper-clipped together.

Officer Hamilton suddenly jumped with a cry as he noticed Brian on his left. Taking a step back and resting his hand on his gun, the officer held his other hand to his chest when he got a look at Brian's hands up. At almost six-foot four in boots, and weighing in at just under 300 pounds, the large man dwarfed the average officer.

"Wow there, big guy!" Hamilton struggled for one breath to get under control. "You scared the SHIT out of me."

Brian shrugged apologetically.

Molly gave him a quick glare, but was very relieved he had arrived. "He walks softly," Molly explained. "Took ballet as a kid."

"Hrm..." Hamilton relaxed, accepted several documents from Molly, and nodded over at Brian. "This your truck?"

"Yes, officer," Brian nodded.

"Pass me your license, too," Hamilton narrowed his eyes.

"You also... carrying? Like your wife here?"

"Yes, officer," he repeated, pointing down to his right side. "Wallet is in the left side pocket. May I get it out?"

"I'll give you the same deal I gave her. Don't show me your gun, and I won't show you mine. Get me your ID. Bunch of truckers carry these days. Don't mind it none as long as there ain't no yelling and shouting."

Brian carefully lowered only his left hand, tugged at a Velcro, and produced ID.

"Okay. Here's how this is gonna work. I'm taking a picture of the GCWR plate on this truck, and then I'll go back to my air-conditioned car and check some things out. I need you two to run this rig through the scales." Hamilton waved at the long line. "Park it over on the right side there, and then wait. I'll be by in a few to verify the read."

"We're well under 26,000, officer," Brian complained as the fuel clicked to completion.

"Issue is, that plus that." Hamilton pointed to the truck and trailer. "Can technically carry just a touch over 13 tons. Since it can, I have to ensure that it's not, as that would require a CDL Class A in this state, even if you're just going camping for fun. And my minor task today is to check everyone through this truck stop."

Brian raised an eyebrow.

"Sorry, boys," Molly pulled out her girl card. "Any chance I can go pee while he gets in line?"

Hamilton and Brian exchanged glances, and the officer motioned towards the store. "Go on, I've got your ID, miss."

As Molly was walking off, she heard Brian stow the fuel nozzle and Hamilton continue scratching on his clipboard.

"So, you let your wife drive your new truck towing this big 5th wheel?"

"Eh," Brian clicked print on the receipt prompt. "She can handle herself with equipment. Molly's spent most of the last few weeks working our tractor laying in a large garden."

Hearing the comment, Molly shouted in reflex over her shoulder. "MY tractor, Navy! Get it right!"

Hamilton, laughing his ass off, walked towards the idling SUV parked off to the side of the pumps. Brian moved into the scale line but kept his eyes out towards the store for his... *Friend? Girlfriend? But not his wife.*

"Hrm," Brian sniffed, feeling a sudden strike of emotions at his core. "Maybe?"

Brian moved the rig up one slot in the line of eight trucks at the scales. Then the next guy in line had to pause as the driver who had just scaled stalked off to the DOT officer's car with a mad expression on his face which translated down to the stomping of his flip-flops on the hot asphalt. With a sigh, Brian reached back and snagged the open Moxie from the cup holder in the back.

Lights went off on a little black box, not much bigger than a radar detector mounted with some strong tape on the dash. First two red, then seven red. Then the entire set of ten lit and flashed back and forth.

The little plastic rectangle was wired into a larger RDI produced radio system called a BattleBox. It was a sort of grab-bag-do-it-all communications ad hoc network system with all kinds of abilities to coordinate, control and command hundreds of connected devices. The little add-on attached with adhesive to his dashboard, with several complaints about it at the time from him on his newish used truck, was a recent addition to the expansion capabilities of the BattleBox. The rectangle, and the software application running it, Brian was told, were to detect attempts at tracking or, worse, active attacks on the devices connected to the Box. This included both his and Molly's cellphones, the Wi-Fi devices in the camper, the smart TV, and even the wireless backup camera Molly had the foresight to overnight to them when they went to pickup the camper from Kentucky the two days before.

"Hrm," Brian stared at the lights of the little box, which was obviously mad about something. Then he felt a buzz from his phone. He looked at the notification, sent internally from the BattleBox software. In the message were two words. *Attack Detected!*

Brian looked left and noticed a silver minivan pull around the corner at speed. It squeaked to a halt across two handicap spots right next to the trucker's entrance to the gas station. Four men with shotguns got out and moved into a stack on the door.

"NO!" Brian cried. "Not again!"

He yanked his plate carrier from under a blanket in the back seat, tossed Molly's rifle over his left shoulder, and exited the idling truck at a run with his Tavor X95 sling dropping over his head.

Check https://kendecoteau.com/ for updates on the upcoming Fall 2025 release date of *From the Ashes,* and other novels in the universe.